COLLECTION MANAGEMENT

3/11	3 - 1	1/11

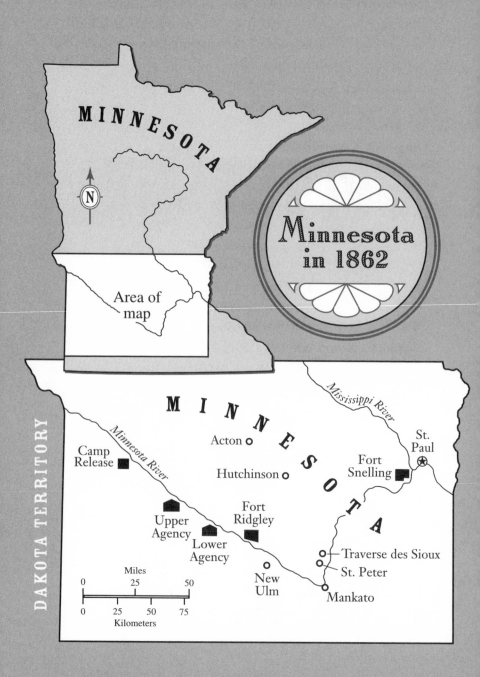

BATTLE CRY

JAN
NEUBERT
SCHULTZ

Carolrhoda Books, Inc. • Minneapolis

This book is dedicated to my mentor,
Mary Casanova,
with deep gratitude and affection.

Text copyright © 2006 by Jan Neubert Schultz
Cover illustration copyright © 2006 by Rick Allen
Map on p. 2 by Laura Westlund, copyright © 2006 by Carolrhoda Books, Inc.

Carolrhoda Books, Inc.
A division of Lerner Publishing Group
241 First Avenue North
Minneapolis, MN 55401 U.S.A.

Website address: www.lernerbooks.com

Library of Congress Cataloging-in-Publication Data

Schultz, Jan Neubert.
    Battle cry / by Jan Neubert Schultz.
        p. cm.
    Summary: In 1862, two best friends, one white and one half Dakota Indian, find themselves involved in a bloody war when when the Dakotas, fed up with being mistreated by the federal government and local citizens, erupt with violence.
    ISBN-13: 978-1-57505-928-0 (lib. bdg. : alk. paper)
    ISBN-10: 1-57505-928-2 (lib. bdg. : alk. paper)
    1. Dakota Indians—Wars, 1862-1865—Juvenile fiction. [1. Dakota Indians—Wars, 1862-1865—Fiction. 2. Indians of North America—Minnesota—Fiction. 3. Best friends—Fiction. 4. Friendship—Fiction. 5. Frontier and pioneer life—Minnesota—Fiction. 6. Minnesota—History—1858—-Fiction.] I. Title.
    PZ7.S3885Bat 2006
    [Fic]—dc22   2005024095

Manufactured in the United States of America
1 2 3 4 5 6 – BP – 11 10 09 08 07 06

YA Fic

CONTENTS

AUTHOR'S NOTE

Battle Cry is a work of fiction, set against the Dakota Conflict of 1862. All efforts have been made to accurately portray events, an exception being the battle of New Ulm and the battle of Fort Ridgely, which are condensed in this book; New Ulm and Fort Ridgley each fought off two attacks. The Dakota Conflict was widespread, lasted over six weeks, and included many more events than those portrayed in this book.

Johnny Preuss, Ma, Pa, and Amy are fictional characters, as is Chaska (pronounced CHAS-kay). Their words and actions are fictional. John Other Day is a historical character. He was married to a white woman, and they had a son, on whom the fictional character Chaska is based. Agent Galbraith, Andrew Myrick, and all others are historical characters, crafted in word and action through research, using first-person accounts whenever possible to portray them accurately.

The Native Americans in this story are referred to by two names. Dakota, the name by which they call themselves, means "friends" or "allies." The Chippewa (now known as Ojibwa), traditional enemies of the Dakota, called them Sioux, meaning "snakelike" or "enemy." This derogatory term came into common usage. Except for place-names and historical usage, the correct term *Dakota* is used in this book.

FOREWORD

During the 1850s, the Dakota were in hard straits brought on by successive crop failures and depletion of game in the forests. They faced severe hardships and starvation.

On July 23, 1851, the Wahpeton and Sisseton, northern bands of the Upper Sioux area, ceded their lands to the United States for $1,665,000 in cash and annuities. On August 5, 1851, the Mdewakanton and Wahpekute, southern bands of the Lower Sioux area, signed away their lands for $1,410,000 in cash and annuities over a fifty-year period. In all, the Dakota Nation ceded nearly 24,000,000 acres of land, which was soon opened to white settlement.

The Dakota were given reservation lands, administered by federal government agencies. They were assured by Governor Ramsey that they had made a good treaty. The Great White Father would always watch over his red children.

But the United States Congress changed the terms of the treaty, greatly lessening the payments and goods the Dakota had been promised. And when the annuities arrived, they were first distributed to the unscrupulous traders and agents, who took what they claimed the Dakota owed them for goods charged in their stores.

The Dakota on the reservations were urged to take up white ways—to farm and to cut their hair short. In return, they were given houses and 40 acres. Those who did were called "farmer Indians." Their reservation brothers, who determined to hold to their ways, were called "blanket Indians."

By the summer of 1862, there was widespread unrest among the Dakota. They didn't have enough food for their families. They needed blankets, guns, and ammunition to hunt. Their annuity had not arrived, and they feared the government had spent all the annuity money and goods funding the Civil War.

Times were tense and tempers were short. The Dakota were desperate.

"They Can Eat Grass"
August 16, 1862

Johnny braced his back against the papery white bark of the birch, eased his rifle against his shoulder, and tilted his head to the small-notched sight. Antlers merged with willow twigs. Johnny hesitated, waiting for movement from the buck, but it stood motionless.

Early morning sunlight crept down the ravine slope, shadows and light dappling the blurry images. Johnny stepped right, the crunch of dry leaves underfoot muffled by the rushing of the anxious creek. A smile rippled across his face—Chaska had found a deer and had driven it Johnny's way. Johnny scanned the willows for dark deer hide against white bark.

There? He brought his rifle up to his cheek.

CRACK! A shot rang out—from high on the opposite bank. Squawking, flapping crows erupted from the top branches. The buck pitched forward into the creek, flailing and kicking. A buckskin-clad boy jumped out from behind a rocky outcrop, leapt from log to boulder to creek bed, and splashed through the swirling water.

Johnny raced down to the creek, slipping on loose leaves, sliding on mossy rocks.

"Chaska, you got him!"

Chaska reached the deer, grabbed an antler, and pulled the buck's head up and back. "We hunt together. We got him!" Chaska laughed, waving Johnny across the creek. "The mighty hunters strike again." With a quick slash of his hunting knife, blood and life spurted into the stream, eddied around a clutch of river rocks, and flowed away downstream.

Johnny sloshed through knee-deep water and stopped in front of Chaska and the buck. Reddish water swirled around and into Johnny's boots. Reaching down, he grabbed the deer's near antler and helped flip the heavy animal onto the creek bank. "He's huge. Most deer around here are skinny. Do you suppose he came up from Iowa Territory?"

Chaska slipped a rope noose around the base of the antlers. "Could be. I hope he brought friends." He grinned as he threw the rope over a tall elm alongside the creek.

Johnny caught it as it fell. Together they hoisted the heavy carcass off the ground, and secured the rope around the tree trunk.

A warm blood smell hung heavy in the air as

Chaska's skinning knife slit the deer's white belly. A slight gust shook dry yellow leaves off the willows, and they whirled down. Johnny watched Chaska's sure, steady motions.

Laying his knife on the ground, Chaska reached his hands into the deer's chest cavity, pulling out and down, drawing out the heart, lungs, liver, entrails. All the while Chaska muttered thanks to the slain animal for its gift of life and strength to him and his people. The deer swayed as he worked, and Johnny steadied it from the back. Finished, Chaska took a step over to the creek and splashed handfuls of water into the carcass, swishing it clean. He rinsed the organs and tossed them back into the cavity.

Johnny untied the rope, easing the deer to the ground. "Eight-point buck. Enough meat to feed our families half the winter."

Chaska washed his hands, cleaned his knife, and slipped it into its sheath. "Everyone needs meat. And there's not enough to be had."

"This deer will help." Johnny tied the animal's front legs together; Chaska tied the back. They looked up the steep ravine slope, then at each other. "We'll have to drag it," said Johnny. Grasping the deer's bound legs, the boys hauled it uphill. Reaching the rim, they swung the deer in an arc, heaving it to the top, where it landed with a wet thud on level ground.

Johnny stepped out of the dim damp woods into hot bright meadow. He wiped his arm across his face, the homespun sleeve already wet with sweat. Johnny brushed his brown hair off his brow and looked at Chaska leaning against a tree trunk. His hair was neatly braided. His dark eyes were sharp and clear. No trace of sweat on his bare chest. Not even breathing hard.

Johnny shoved the buck with his foot. "Let's get going. It's a long way home."

"First we go to the reservation." Chaska whistled for Lightfoot, his pinto, grazing nearby. "We'll leave my half there, then take the other half to your farm."

"That's a far piece. Can't the reservation Indians do their own hunting?" Then Johnny bit his tongue, remembering Chaska's grandmother and cousin lived in the Dakota village.

Irritation crept into Chaska's voice. "There's not so much as a rabbit left alive anywhere near the reservation." He bent and lifted the carcass, tossing it over Lightfoot's steady back.

Johnny helped position the deer from Lightfoot's other side. "Then they should farm—raise cattle and crops—instead of waiting for their annuities."

Chaska stared at Johnny across the horse's back. Sweaty horse smell and pungent carcass odor wafted up between them. "You know those annuities are payment for the land the government took from them. That's how they buy their supplies." He leapt onto the pinto behind the buck and cantered off.

Johnny ran to get his saddled horse, which was tied in a grove of trees, and galloped after Chaska. Caught up, he glanced at Chaska's tight-lipped mouth. He didn't understand why Chaska was so touchy. It had been over ten years since the Dakota had sold their land to the government. It was about time the Dakota adjusted, adapted.

Slowing to an easy trot, Chaska looked over at Johnny. "The women grow corn, but the Dakota are not farmers," he said, his tone softer. "Always they've hunted and lived off the land. And now the land belongs to the whites."

"But your father farms. Other Day is a respected warrior, yet he farms. You have a house and barn and livestock and cropland. You cut your hair and wear white man's clothes."

Chaska looked away, not answering. Johnny frowned, confused. Did Chaska have a problem with his father's choices? No, that couldn't be. Chaska admired his father. He dearly loved his white mother. Johnny and Chaska had grown up together on adjoining farms, best friends, their families more like relatives than neighbors. Yet lately Johnny noticed Chaska went to the reservation a lot. He had joined a Warrior's Lodge, whatever that was. He wore buckskins whenever he hunted. It seemed like he favored reservation life over the farm. Like he'd rather live there. Johnny wasn't sure what to think. Would Chaska rather be with the Dakota boys than with him?

"It would do you no good to go back to the reservation," Johnny blurted out. "Whites are here to stay. We have to live together. . . ."

Chaska pulled Lightfoot up short, blocking Johnny. "Whites don't want to live together with Indians. Whites intend to destroy the Dakota's ways." He jerked Lightfoot's rein away, galloping him through a stand of birches.

Johnny spurred his horse after him, puzzled by Chaska's intense reaction. Johnny stayed a respectful distance behind. He thought it best he keep his mouth shut for awhile.

The horses slowed to an easy trot as they approached the wooded reservation land. Tall elms canopied leafy branches across the dirt lane, and Johnny was glad for the coolness they offered. Splashing across a shallow river ford, they entered the Dakota village. They rode down neat rows of teepees, bustling with women tending stew pots, sewing tanned hides, washing clay utensils at river's edge. A group of children played lacrosse, tossing rocks from netted rawhide racquets, running and shouting.

Chaska turned around on his horse, scanning the village. "Where are the braves?"

"Chaska!" hollered a small boy. Rocks and racquets dropped into the dust as children raced over, crowding around the horses. "Deer! Chaska brings deer!"

With a brisk headshake, Chaska motioned them aside, heading toward the last teepee in the row. Johnny followed, the children bounding along behind.

Sitting outside her teepee flap, Chaska's grandmother ground boiled acorns into a handful of meal. She smiled up at the approaching boys, her eyes crinkling, then widening at the sight of the deer. A girl about their same age quickly slipped inside the teepee.

"Greetings, Grandmother," called Chaska. "We had a good hunt. The Great Spirit provided meat."

"Greetings, Star Woman," Johnny said in Dakota, glad that Chaska had taught him their language. "And to you, Raven." The girl, Chaska's cousin, had come out of the teepee carrying a skinning knife. She smiled distractedly at Chaska and Johnny, her attention riveted on the deer.

Chaska slipped off his pony, grasped the hindquarters of the deer, and lowered it to the ground alongside the teepee. Raven grasped the rope still around its antlers and tossed it over an elm branch. Johnny jumped off his own horse to help hoist the deer, struggling a bit as the children shoved closer. From behind, a woman's sharp voice barked a command. The eager youngsters fell back silent, and Johnny glanced around. Every woman in the village had gathered, each with a knife and birch-bark basket. They stood back, waiting a turn.

Raven tossed her long, black braids over her shoulders and slid a knife between the deer's hide and muscle, drawing the blade in short strokes, separating skin from meat. Chaska carved a shoulder from the front haunch and glanced at Johnny, inviting him to cut out his share.

Johnny looked at all the pinched, eager faces, at the skinny arms and legs of the children. Chaska was right; it had been a long time since anyone had had enough to eat.

Johnny shook his head, no.

Chaska tossed the venison chunk into his grandmother's cook pot. "Where are all the braves?" He motioned to the large teepee at the center of the encampment, the Warrior's Lodge. No smoke curled out of the open tip. No horses tethered nearby. "Have they gone on a hunt? I should have been told."

"Where would they hunt? What would they hunt?" muttered Star Woman. She waved a hand as if to sweep her words away. "They are at the Lower Sioux Agency. They say they will get wheat today. If they don't, we won't survive the winter."

"We must go," said Chaska. Exchanging anxious glances, the boys remounted and rode up a hilly wooded lane, coming out onto a large prairie-grass meadow. A path connected the scattered houses and cabins where the settlement people lived and worked. They passed a carpentry shop, a granary, Dr. Daniel's cottage, and Dr. Humphrey's white frame house. No one seemed to be around. Everyone's doors were shut, but thin curls of smoke eddied up from chimneys. Chaska nudged his pony's flanks, hurrying him along. Johnny kept pace alongside him, dust rising in their wake.

Their horses' ears pricked forward, their heads held higher. Suddenly, Johnny and Chaska could hear angry voices, in English and Dakota, from across the grassy expanse. "That's coming from the warehouse," said Chaska, urging Lightfoot to a canter.

At the center of the settlement loomed an imposing stone warehouse, where Indian Agent Galbraith had his office. From there, he dispensed the Dakota's annual annuity goods—blankets, guns and ammunition, kettles and knives, foodstuffs—and the gold payment.

Lots of men had gathered, their arms waving, some fist-shaking. "Looks like there's trouble," said Chaska, halting his pony. "I'd been afraid of that." Johnny stopped too, trying to see what was happening.

Traders and shopkeepers in white homespun shirts and dark suspendered pants stood on the wide stone platform that fronted the warehouse, shouting in the angry faces of leather-clad Dakota standing in front of them on the grass. The Dakota shoved their way toward the big bolted doors set deep in the stone walls. A bloc of navy-blue uniformed soldiers barricaded the doorway, their rifles gripped across their chests.

A bearded man in a frock coat went to the center of the platform, plunked down a square wooden box, and stood on it. He shouted for order, speaking Dakota. "That's Agent Galbraith," said Chaska, his voice tight.

Agent Galbraith pulled his black hat down to shade his narrow eyes, smoothed his black goatee with one hand, and scanned the angry crowd. He rapped the box sharply with his cane and shouted again, his deep voice demanding attention.

Chaska snorted. "Thinks he's the Great White Father himself."

"Nothing will be dispersed today!" Galbraith shouted, triggering an angry roar.

"You have our food! Our grain!" A brave's bare-fisted arm shot up, punching the air as his words did. "Give it to us—it is ours by right!"

Galbraith aimed a pointed finger at the gesturing brave. "The food won't be distributed until the gold gets here. You'll get your food allotment when your gold allotment arrives. I'm only going to do the hand-outs one time!"

The braves surged forward. They stopped suddenly when the soldiers raised their rifles and aimed into the Dakota's faces and chests.

Chief Little Crow stepped forward. "You promised us that provisions would be given us. Now you will not give them." Taking a step closer to Agent Galbraith, he said, "Then tell the traders they must give us credit to buy food from them." The braves edged closer, muttering among themselves.

Galbraith crossed his arms over his chest, scanned the restless crowd, and called over to the adjacent trader's store. "Trader Myrick, will you extend credit?"

Silence dropped like a boulder in soft dust. All eyes turned to the trader, leaning against his porch post, one booted foot on the railing. He spat a stream of tobacco juice into the dirt. "They can eat grass. Or their own dung." He stomped into his store and slammed the door shut.

Johnny's mouth dropped open. He glanced at Chaska, whose angry face seemed carved in stone. A stunned hush smothered the clearing.

Agent Galbraith's jaws clamped shut. He jumped off his box and hustled into the the warehouse, slamming the door behind him. Loud clangs echoed as iron bolts were shoved into place. The other traders hurriedly left to close their stores. The soldiers fanned out in front of the warehouse, their bayoneted rifles still aimed at the Dakota.

The braves huddled. The soldiers stood fast, guns steady, individual braves in their sights. Then, like a sudden rumbling rock slide, the braves leapt onto their horses and galloped out of the clearing.

Cold goose flesh rippled down Johnny's arm. How could Agent Galbraith refuse to give the grain when it stood in the warehouse? And trader Myrick! Eat grass or dung? He reached his hand out to Chaska. How would the Dakota survive?

Without a word, without a glance, Chaska kicked his pony in the ribs and raced after the braves. "Chaska!" Johnny stood in his stirrups, trying to see. Why was Chaska going after them? Should he follow? "Come back!" he yelled. His startled horse reared, and Johnny quickly reined him down. When would he see Chaska again?

INCIDENT AT ACTON
August 17, 1862

Johnny thumped his hatchet into the chopping block and picked up the kindling wood for Ma's cookstove. He'd hurried through morning chores, hoping to catch up with Chaska later in the day. He hadn't seen him since they'd been at the Agency the day before.

The barn door slammed shut, and Johnny straightened up to see Amy coming toward him with a bucket of milk from their cow, Old Bessie. At twelve years old, his sister was starting to look all grown up, her blond hair in braids wound around her head, walking all graceful.

But a frown furrowed Amy's face, wrinkling her brow. "Cows are supposed to be gentle, to enjoy being milked. Not ours! We should call her Old Bossy."

Laughing, Johnny sprinted for the cabin. "Race you to the kitchen," he called over his shoulder. Knowing, of course, Amy couldn't run with a full milk pail. He scuttled into one of the bow-back chairs by the table, next to Pa. Amy came in and poured milk into three cups, seeming to forget Johnny's, then turned back to the woodstove to help Ma with breakfast.

Pa reached for the platter of fried eggs and bacon, the savory aroma steaming across the table. "Johnny, hitch the horses after breakfast. We'll go to Acton Township. I've got an order to take a load of supplies to Jones's store."

Ma looked up quickly. "On a Sunday?"

"I wanted to hunt with Chaska," said Johnny.

"Can't be helped," said Pa, an edge to his voice. "Tomorrow I start at Fort Ridgely, building barracks all next week."

Ma turned back to the stove, banging a few kettles as she dished up oatmeal.

~~~

By midday, Pa and Johnny were well on the way to Acton. It was a warm summer day, grasshoppers dancing in and out of the cornrows alongside the road. The horses' hooves clopped up little whirlwinds of dust. Suddenly Johnny cocked his head. "Pa, hear that? What's that ruckus up ahead?"

"Hollering? Crying?" asked Pa, urging the horses into a canter. He swung off the road onto a dirt lane that led to a cleared farmstead with a neat log cabin in its center. Johnny stood on the wagon seat, glancing frantically around. Where was that God-awful howl coming from? It sounded like someone trying not to die.

At the clearing's far edge, he spotted a woman kneeling on the ground, rocking back and forth. She was crouched over something on the ground. No, someone. A man, it looked like. Was he hurt? Had there been some sort of accident? Pa spoke sharp to the skittish horses, tightening the reins. Johnny jumped off the wagon and raced through the long grass to the woman and knelt beside her.

The man sure was dead. There was a big hole in his chest and way too much blood. Johnny leaned back on his heels, not sure what to do next. The woman didn't seem to realize anyone was beside her.

Pa got off the wagon and came toward Johnny, but suddenly he veered away. Johnny left the distraught woman and ran after him. Pa bent down over another man lying in the grass, grasped his shoulders, and rolled him over. Johnny leaned forward slightly, shuddering as blood ran out of an open wound and puddled in the grass. He was dead, too. Gunshot?

"What's happened here?" Pa shouted back to the crying woman. He and Johnny ran over to her.

Startled, she looked up at Pa. Sobbing and hiccuping, she gulped out an answer. "All killed! All killed!"

"Who shot them?" asked Johnny. "Did they shoot each other? Was there an argument?" The woman straightened up and turned to Johnny. He stopped dead in his tracks. She clutched a baby!

The wide-eyed woman gripped her thumb-sucking infant. Huddling the child close, looking one way and another, she searched the clearing. "Indians. It was Indians."

Johnny figured she'd gone crazy. She certainly looked crazy. Indians didn't kill for no reason. Her words rushed out in a torrent. "Four Indians come by and were target shooting with the menfolk, by yonder tree, all friendlylike." Her voice pitched higher, frantic. "Suddenly they turned and shot everyone! My husband here, Mr. Baker. And his mother, Mrs. Jones, and Mr. Jones. Then Mr. Webster!" She looked desperately from one body to another, and Johnny saw there were more in the tall grass. "Thank heavens I was still in the cabin. I hid in the cellar with my baby," she whispered, crooning now to the very quiet child. Suddenly she screamed, "Where's Mrs. Webster?"

Pa stooped down and put his hand on the woman's shoulder to calm her. "Johnny," he said softly, "check the covered wagon under those elms."

Johnny raced to the wagon and leaned over the end gate. He shifted a heaped mound of quilts, loosing a piercing scream from underneath. He jumped back, nearly jumped out of his skin. "What in blazes? Who's there?" he yelled.

A young woman's head stuck out from under a bright colorful quilt, her hair sticking up every which way. "Are they gone?" she shrieked. "They shot my husband! We only just got married last month, and they killed him!" She scurried out of the wagon box and ran to the bodies by the tree, dropping down beside a bloody corpse. "We should have stayed in Wisconsin! Indians here are killers!"

Indians again, thought Johnny. He looked at Pa in dismay. It couldn't be so.

Pa was struggling to get Mrs. Baker and her baby up onto the wagon seat. He motioned Johnny to go get Mrs. Webster. Johnny went to the woman, crouched on the ground and cradling her husband's bloody head. He tapped her shoulder. "We have to go now." She wouldn't move. Johnny took both her shoulders in his hands and tugged. "We have to go," he repeated, voice insistent. "We'll bring everyone with us. Come to the wagon."

She calmed a bit, hearing a strong male voice, and she stood up. Hands still on her shoulders, Johnny steered her toward the wagon. Pa took her elbow, edged her to the metal step. "Up you go," he said. She climbed up and sat. Mrs. Baker sat beside her, whimpering over her baby. "Help me carry the others," Pa whispered to Johnny.

They gathered the bodies of Mr. Webster and Mr. Baker, first one and then another. Pa lifted shoulders; Johnny took their knees. They struggled to lay them quietly into the wagon box. Mrs. Baker jumped when she felt and heard the thuds. "Mother Jones and Mr. Jones came over here from their store, just down the lane, and the Indians followed them." Suddenly her hand flew up to her mouth. "The children! Their daughter Clara, and their baby. They're still back at the store." She threw her head back and wailed at the heavens.

"We need to get over there right quick," said Pa, running to the grassy clumps where Mr. and Mrs. Jones lay. Johnny and Pa quickly loaded the bodies. The horses needed no urging; they seemed glad to leave the farmstead and the blood smell.

Johnny knelt behind Pa, in back of the wagon seat. "But Indians, Pa?" he whispered. "Indians around here aren't killers." He kept brushing his arms to make the hairs lie back down.

Pa shook his head. "I can't puzzle it out. Unless they were renegades. Maybe we'll learn more at Jones's store." He gave the reins an unnecessary slap over the horses' backs. "Let's hope to God the killers didn't go back there."

After a half mile of quick jouncing travel, Pa pulled into another clearing. They all sat quiet, scanning the home site. It was silent as a graveyard, not even birdsong. "Looks deserted," said Johnny. "No one's here anymore." He jumped off the wagon, walking briskly toward the log store. A wide verandah stretched across the front, a few tended wildflowers along its edge. He slowed, looking in all directions, especially at the tall meadow grass bordering the clearing.

"There's Clara! Lying in the doorway!" screeched Mrs. Baker, pointing at the cabin porch. "They killed her, too." She reached across Pa to the iron seat rail as if to get down, clutching the baby with one arm. Pa grabbed her other arm and held her in place.

Johnny ran to the verandah and knelt beside the girl sprawled facedown in the doorway. Gently he took her shoulder and turned her toward him, so she rested on his knees. A gunshot wound had punctured her chest. She was about Amy's age. And she had blond braids, wet with blood.

"You can't help her no more," yelled Pa. "Look inside for a baby." Mrs. Baker struggled against Pa's hold on her arm.

Johnny tried to wipe the blood off Clara's face, smearing it. He took a deep gasping breath and had to gulp it down.

"Johnny!" Pa hollered. "Leave her! Look for the baby. Now!"

Johnny shook his head to clear it. He lay the girl down gently, as if afraid to hurt her more. He rose and stepped into the dim interior of the cabin-store, the wood floorboards creaking under his boots. He heard a whimper, a tiny squeak. There, in a dark corner, a cradle rocked. Small arms reached up, little hands grasped at air. Johnny peered into the carved cradle at a wiggly blue bundle. A little round face, tear-streaked, pleaded up at him. Johnny lifted the baby out, and its small arms tightened around his neck.

Johnny held the baby close, patted its back, rubbed its arms and legs, and smoothed its hair. The whimpers quieted, and the baby began to squirm a bit. "Hey baby," Johnny said softly. "You're not hurt. You're all right."

He swayed back and forth, rocking the baby. Finally he realized Pa was calling him, sounding frantic. Johnny carried the baby to the doorway. He stopped and stared down at Clara.

"That baby all right?" yelled Pa. "Bring it over here, right now."

Johnny stepped carefully over Clara and walked to the wagon. Mrs. Baker was sitting quieter, now gripping her baby instead of Pa's arm. Mrs. Webster was groaning softly.

Pa reached for the baby Johnny held, and it went to him willingly. "Can you carry the girl to the wagon by yourself?"

Nodding yes, Johnny went back to Clara, knelt down, and eased his arms under her, lifting her like a sleeping child. Her head rolled against his chest and rested there. The soft thud nearly made his own heart stop.

"Easy does it," said Pa gently. Johnny took a deep shuddering breath and carried the girl to the wagon, laying her beside Mrs. Jones. There were blankets in the load of supplies, and Johnny unfolded one and tucked it around Clara. He laid another blanket over the other bodies, too.

Taking the baby back from Pa, Johnny settled himself behind the wagon seat. The baby wanted to crawl, and Johnny had to talk to him and bounce him on his lap to keep him from squirming away. He couldn't let him go to those blankets.

"Can you reach the rifle if we need it?" Pa whispered over his shoulder.

What? Need it? Might the killers still be around here? Johnny looked from Pa's grim face to the gun under the wagon seat. He reached for the rifle and laid it beside him. "Got it," he said, his voice a croak. "Where're we going?"

"Forest City is nearby. There'll be folks there to care for these women and children. Besides, we need to alert them there are renegade Indians nearby."

It didn't take long to reach Forest City, a small village with a tree-lined front street. Pa pulled up to a hitching rail in front of the general store and yelled for help. In seconds, villagers swarmed out of stores and homes, quickly surrounding the wagon. They pulled back the blankets. "What in God's name happened? Where'd you find these folks? Who shot them? Robbers? Horse thieves?"

Mrs. Webster and Mrs. Baker and her baby all started crying at once, which set the baby Johnny held a-crying, too. Ladies quickly hustled them off the wagons and inside the nearest house. A black-bonneted lady took the baby Johnny was holding. Pa lowered the end gate to carry the slain settlers inside.

Johnny took Clara in his arms again, carried her inside, and lay her on a bed, where a quilt covered a straw mattress. He threw a knitted shawl over her chest to hide the dreadful wound, straightened her braids, and started to wipe her face with a corner of the sheeting.

A short plump lady, her voice as soft as Ma's, took

the cloth from him. "We'll take care of her now," she said. Taking Johnny's arm, she steered him gently but firmly toward the door. "She's got kinfolk here who'll tend to her."

Johnny walked slowly to the wagon, where Pa waited for him. It seemed like he should say good-bye to Clara, do something more for her. It didn't seem right to just leave her there.

"I Am Not a Coward"

Late night, August 17, 1862

Johnny touched match to wick and hung the lantern on a tenpenny nail by the horse stall. Evening chores were long finished and dark shadows settled deep in the corners of the barn, but Johnny didn't want to go back to the cabin yet. If Chaska came, he wanted to talk to him alone. Pa had told Other Day what they'd seen at Acton, and Other Day and Chaska had gone to the Agency to investigate. That had been long hours ago. What was keeping them?

The animals, fed and watered, bedded down for the night. Old Bessie settled herself with a rustle of straw and chewed her cud. Looking around for more to do, Johnny grabbed the currycomb. The horses were not used to grooming at this time of night. His bay gelding edged away as Johnny bore down with the stiff brush.

Finally, Johnny heard the sound of hoofbeats outside. He grabbed the leather latch and pulled open the barn door.

Chaska cantered right in, pulled his pony up short, and slid off its sweat-sleeked back. He was alone, wearing his leather leggings and moccasins. Squatting beside Lightfoot, Chaska traced his hands along the horse's legs and fetlocks. "We've been running hard." Swiveling on his heels, he looked up at Johnny. "A lot has happened. All bad."

Johnny stared at Chaska, slightly silhouetted by the scant moonlight coming through the door. Worse than the killings at Acton?

"The settlers at Acton were killed by four braves from Rice Creek, Red Middle Voice's village. They were hunting in this area and happened by Jones's store. They noticed a hen's nest along a fence line and argued about whether to steal the eggs. One called another a coward, afraid to steal an egg from a white man. To prove to each other they were not cowards, they went to the cabin and killed the settlers."

Johnny bit his lip. "They killed a woman and a girl. How brave is that?"

"I suppose they didn't want anyone to identify them." Chaska stood deep in the shadows. "They went back to their village and bragged about their bravery and their stolen horses. A council of chiefs met that same night, to decide what actions they should take."

"Was Other Day there?"

"No, but I was. At the war council at Little Crow's house."

A chill traced down Johnny's spine as he remembered the pent-up fury of the braves at the Agency warehouse. But at least the marauding Indians were not from this area. They could be caught before anything else happened. And Chief Little Crow was fair and influential. He wouldn't condone this killing.

"The younger braves demanded they go to war. They said that because of the killings, there will be reprisals against all the tribes. And that now the government will never give out the annuities."

"War? Murder doesn't need to lead to war! How can they even consider war as a solution? Think of the consequences!"

Chaska sat on the straw-strewn floor and crossed his legs, as if he were still at the council. Johnny sat facing him. "Johnny, you think for a minute. The Dakota have been cheated out of what was promised them ever since they signed the treaty. When their annuities arrive, the traders help themselves to the goods and to the gold coins. The Indian agents steal from them as well."

The flickering lantern light reflected off their faces; Chaska's tense, Johnny's scared. "They steal from the Dakota? They take the money and the goods?"

"Johnny, you see they have nothing. You heard

Agent Galbraith refuse to give them the food that was in the warehouse. And you heard Myrick refuse them credit. Remember what he said?"

Dread trickled down Johnny's back, raising goose bumps. "They could eat grass or their own dung." He shuddered in the dark. He remembered the women and children in Star Woman's village, near to starving.

"Year after year, they endure hardship and scorn, cheating and lying. Nothing will change," said Chaska. "The Dakota have just cause. If not the Acton murders, another incident will start a war. A war of survival."

"But, Chaska, there's no chance they could win a war against the U.S. Army."

"The braves gave good reasons why such a war could be won. First of all, the white soldiers are nearly all gone, fighting the Great War in the South. Because of that, the Dakota braves think that the northern bands, the Sisseton and the Lakota, will join them. That even the Winnebago and the Ojibwa would join in a war against the whites. There would be enough warriors to defeat the white soldiers still here."

"Do you think that, too?" Johnny wanted to know where Chaska stood.

Chaska shrugged, not giving a direct answer. "The chiefs argued against war. Little Crow told them that the white men would return faster than they could count them, and with guns to kill them. Chief Wabasha and Chief Big Eagle said too that they'd be defeated, that they'd be driven off all the land, even their reservations. Traveling Hail pointed out that they have no ammunition and that the whites have cannons."

Johnny's heartbeat slowed a bit. "Reasonable arguments from honored chiefs."

Chaska looked around the dark barn as if he were still in the war council. "Neither side could convince the other. The braves are intent on war, the chiefs advise against it." He was quiet a moment, as though still listening to the chiefs. "They would not agree. They are divided, the war party against the peace party."

Johnny reached over and touched Chaska's arm. "What will happen? Who decides?"

Chaska stood and brushed straw shreds from his leggings. "Little Crow does. He told the young warriors that they were fools. That they were full of the white men's whiskey. That making war was madness and they should heed their chiefs."

Johnny stood, too, with a sigh of relief. "Thank God for Little Crow."

"That wasn't the end of it. The braves threatened to go to war in spite of the chief's decision. Little Crow rubbed black ashes on his face, as if he were mourning, and covered his head with a blanket."

Johnny held his breath. Where was all this leading?

"It was silent for a long time; no one sure what to think or what to say. Finally, one furious warrior said Little Crow was afraid to fight. He called Little Crow a coward."

Chaska reached for Lightfoot's reins, leading him to the doorway. "That is a terrible insult to a great chief, a great tribal leader."

Johnny followed, sweat trickling down his back.

Chaska's voice deepened, reverberating off the high rafters, ricocheting off the cavernous wooden walls. "Little Crow threw aside his covering, stood, and swiped the young warrior's eagle-feathered headdress off his head. He spoke like a chief; he said, 'Little Crow is not a coward! And he is not a fool! When did he run away from his enemies? Look at his war feathers! Look at the scalps of his enemies hanging on his lodge poles! Braves, you are like children. You are like dogs in the Hot Moon when they run mad and snap at their own shadows.'"

Clouds darkened the moon, and Chaska's form as well. "He said, 'Little Crow is not a coward! He will die with you!'"

Johnny stared at Chaska, seeing only a dim shadow. He struggled to absorb Little Crow's decision. Little

Crow would lead a war against the whites?

Chaska leapt onto Lightfoot. "Little Crow will lead the war party. No one knows yet what the peace party will do. The attacks begin at dawn. Take your family to Fort Ridgely." He kicked Lightfoot in the flanks and raced out the barn door. The night wind swept his words away.

"Wait!" said Johnny, running after. "Where are you . . . "

"Don't delay!" yelled Chaska, as he disappeared into the ravenous night.

Johnny's knees nearly gave way; he grasped the door frame for support. Fear flapped around his head like bats swooping from the dark rafters. Attacks at dawn? Dear God, would his family be threatened? And what would become of Chaska? His father was a Dakota warrior, his mother a white woman. What would Chaska do if war broke out?

ON THE WARPATH
Early morning, August 18, 1862

Squinting into the rising sun, Johnny slapped the reins against the horses' backs. Old Bessie, tied to the rear of the wagon, bellowed in protest at the change of pace. "We're almost there, Bessie," said Johnny.

Amy scrambled out of her nest of blankets in the buckboard and stood behind the wagon seat, peering between Pa's and Johnny's shoulders. Sunrise silhouetted a scattering of buildings. "Is that it? That's no fort. There's no stockade."

"That's it," said Pa. He held his rifle across his lap.

Ma, sitting between them, leaned ahead as if to see better. "But there's soldiers there to protect us. Isn't that so, Pa?" She clutched a linen-wrapped bundle of foodstuffs.

"The Fifth Minnesota is quartered there, about a hundred soldiers. And another twenty-five if Company C is still there."

Passing a row of log cabins surrounding the fort

perimeter, Johnny drove into the large open square of parade ground ringed by painted wood frame buildings. To his left, soldiers bustled out of the large two-story stone barracks, evidently headed toward breakfast. "Turn right," Pa directed. "Headquarters is over yonder." He pointed out a large white building on the south side of the parade ground, two separate wings joined by a central hallway, all fronted by a wide verandah. "We'll see the commanding officer, tell him about Acton, and offer our help to set up the defenses." Johnny pulled up to the hitching rail, jumped down, and tied the horses.

"Dr. Mueller's quarters are the right side of the building," Pa told Ma. "Let him and Eliza know what's been happening." Pa gave Ma a hand and helped her down.

Ma attempted a brave smile. "Eliza and I will get the women organized preparing food, laundry, and nursing items. We'll get it done."

"What about Old Bessie?" Amy clambered off the rear of the wagon. "Where can she stay? She'll need milking." Bessie stretched her neck and bellowed loud enough to wake whatever soldiers weren't up yet. Amy jerked her lead rope. "Shush!"

"The stables are right out back of Headquarters," said Pa. "There should be room for a cow." He bounded up the verandah steps, Johnny following, knocked briskly, and stepped into the commander's office. "Morning, Captain Marsh. This here's my son, Johnny."

The officer working at his desk looked up, startled. "Mr. Preuss. You're here early. We won't start building till after mess and drills." He leaned back in his chair and straightened his dark blue uniform jacket. Sunlight slanted through the window behind him, shedding light onto his desk, the only furniture in the dusty room except a couple of straightback wooden chairs.

"There won't be much carpentry today." Pa pulled the door shut behind him. "The Dakota are on the warpath."

Captain Marsh sat forward in a hurry. "What are you talking about?"

"Indian attacks will begin soon, most likely at the Lower Sioux Agency—that's nearest to Little Crow's village. They might possibly attack settlers, too." Pa strode to Marsh's desk and leaned both hands on it. "We were warned during the night by our Indian neighbors and came here straightaway. You'd best alert the nearby settlers and get word to the Agency agents."

Captain Marsh shoved his chair back and stood before Pa. An angry frown flashed across his face. "That can't be so. We got the Indians some food supplies and everything settled down. The gold will come any day now. You've just been hearing rumors."

Johnny could see the officer didn't like getting orders from Pa. Johnny'd bet he wouldn't be taking them, either.

"It wasn't a rumor I saw in Acton Township yesterday." Pa didn't budge an inch. "Five settlers were killed by Indians from Red Middle Voice's band, including a woman and a child." Marsh's frown deepened, his eyes narrowed.

"We were there and we saw it," said Johnny, crowding up next to Pa. "Saw the bodies, saw the blood."

"Red Middle Voice's band?" The captain glared from Pa to Johnny. "Not from the reservation, then. It must be renegades. Well, that's not the whole Sioux nation on the warpath. Don't go getting folks riled up by your stories."

"The Acton killings probably were an isolated incident," admitted Pa. "But John Other Day's son Chaska was at a council on the reservation where plans were made to attack the Agency. To attack it today. He warned us to come here." Pa was leaning so far across the desk he was practically nose to nose with the captain. "That's direct and reliable information, and you'd be remiss to ignore it."

Johnny flinched. Pa was sure intent on getting the

captain's attention.

"We've been hearing rumors all summer that the Indians would go on the warpath," Captain Marsh argued. "Every time they'd show up at the Agency demanding food, there was talk of war. That's all it is. Talk." He slapped his hand down hard on his desk. "Just talk!"

"Wasn't just talk at Acton!" Johnny burst out. "There were killings!"

Captain Marsh looked as if he'd slap Johnny's face. "Red Middle Voice's band is under the jurisdiction of Fort Snelling. They'll handle it. It's no concern of ours."

Johnny sent Pa a disgusted look. He figured there was no sense arguing with Captain Marsh. You can't tell anything to a man that won't listen. They both turned to walk out.

"You're welcome to stay," Marsh called after them. "You can help us finish building the stables. Lieutenant Sheehan took Company C to Fort Ripley. We're short-handed."

Johnny and Pa exchanged glances. "Shorthanded. That's bad news," said Pa as they stepped out onto the porch.

"Lots more of it coming." Johnny stood on the verandah, pointing across the long parade ground at the open spaces separating widely scattered buildings. "How can anyone defend this outpost? There's no stockade wall. The buildings are all wood, except the stone barracks and commissary. A few flaming arrows could set everything afire."

"That's not the worst of it. There's no well, either. Soldiers fetch water from a spring in the south ravine." Pa shaded his eyes with his hand, scanning all directions.

"Ravines on three sides. Indians could sneak up through them, and no one would see them coming. And now, hardly more than seventy-five solders are left here to defend the fort."

"If homesteads are attacked, more settlers will come here like we did. We won't be entirely defenseless." But Johnny knew it didn't look good. "Isn't there any way to convince Marsh, or anyone else, they had better get ready for attacks?"

"Henry Preuss!" called a voice from the next doorway. "Come in here. What's this your missus is telling us?" A white-haired portly gentleman in a black suit beckoned them inside. Dr. Mueller, Johnny guessed.

Ma, Amy, and Eliza Mueller were already scrubbing and scouring the kitchen table. Dr. Mueller's instruments were laid out by a wainscoted dry sink. A teakettle on the woodstove whistled that the water was boiling.

Ma hustled over to Pa, grasped his arm. "Becky Other Day's not here. Where would John have taken her? She won't be safe out there just because she's married to an Indian."

"I don't rightly know." Pa looked questioningly at Johnny. "Did Chaska say where they would be going?"

A worried frown rippled across Johnny's brow. "No, he didn't. He said what he had to say and left in a hurry." Johnny had been wondering the same thing all night—where had Chaska gone?

"It's true, then?" asked Dr. Muller. "The fort will be attacked?"

"Yes, and time's a-wasting," said Pa. "How can we prepare?"

Eliza ran to her linen cupboard, flung it open, and grabbed all the sheets and towels and tossed them to Ma and Amy. "Start rolling bandages. I'll get the other women that live on the post." She grabbed her bonnet and dashed out the door.

"She should be post commander," commented Johnny, watching Eliza through the doorway, pounding on the doors of the officers' quarters.

Dr. Mueller brushed past him, heading outside. "We'd best talk to the artillery officers." Johnny and Pa hurried after.

"Any sentries on duty?" Johnny bounded down the

steps, stopping suddenly when mountainous dust
clouds rolling along the main road caught his attention.
"Look yonder—wagons coming in. Coming fast!" He
and Pa and the doctor ran to the fort entrance.

From barracks and mess halls and officers' quarters,
shouting people rushed to the gateless entrance, watching the wagon approach. The lathered horses galloped
into the grounds and scattered the onlookers.
"Wounded people here!" hollered the driver, pulling
the horses and wagon to a shuddering halt. Dr. Mueller
climbed the backboard before the dust settled. "Get
stretchers!" he yelled. "Get my medics!" The nearest
soldiers hurried to the dispensary.

Johnny recognized the driver—he ran a boarding-
house at the Lower Agency. "Mr. Dickinson, what happened?"

"Indians!" Mr. Dickinson stood, dropping the reins.
Everyone who had been gaping at the wounded now
crowded around him, all shouting at once. Mr.
Dickinson gasped between breaths, "Indians came in
early, sun barely up, dressed to kill!" He talked fast,
waving his arms. "We didn't think nothing of it at first.
They always paint up. Said they were chasing
Chippewa."

He pointed around the fort buildings as if they were
the Agency buildings. "Soon there was a group of them

around every store, talking like normal to the clerks. Then all of a sudden they started shooting everyone! All over the settlement, all at once, shooting and whooping and screaming. People falling in doorways, running for shelter. Indians chasing after them with tomahawks. We couldn't believe our eyes."

Wiping his forehead with his sleeve, Mr. Dickinson swallowed a deep shuddering breath. "After the first killings, they started looting the stores. That gave us a chance to escape. We ran down through the ravine to the ferry landing, and Charlie ferried us across. He didn't come along with us, though—he stayed with the ferry in case more folks escaped." He turned and stared back down the road as if expecting Charlie to be galloping in. "I sure hope he'll be along right quick."

"I guess we've got a few rampaging Indians on our hands." Captain Marsh's deep commanding voice let everyone know who was in charge. "It can't be too serious." He turned to a very young lieutenant, white-faced with puffy jaws, standing next to him. "Lieutenant Gere, call out the troops. We'll put down these upstarts at the Agency." Marsh shot a determined stare at Johnny, standing alongside. "Do you speak Dakota? Your Pa says you've got Indian neighbors."

"I speak it some," said Johnny, staring back.

"Find Peter Quinn. He's here someplace. The two

of you come along. I'll need translators." Turning his back on Johnny, he yelled in the face of an eager young soldier at his elbow. "Corporal! Ride out after Lieutenant Sheehan. Take my orders that he's to return immediately—that the Indians are raising hell at the Agency." With an air of dismissal, the captain strode off to the stables.

Johnny watched him go. He knew what Marsh really needed was someone who knew how Indians thought and felt and how they might act.

Coming back from the dispensary, Pa had heard Marsh's instructions. He helped saddle Johnny's riding horse, still tied to the back of the buckboard. "It's best I stay here," said Pa, holding the bridle while Johnny tightened the cinch. "Until your group or Lieutenant Sheehan returns, there's less than thirty men left to defend the fort."

"How can Lieutenant Gere be in charge?" Johnny jerked a firm knot in the strap. "He doesn't look twenty years old. And not too healthy-looking, either."

Pa shook his head in disgust. "He's nineteen, three years older than you, and sick with the mumps." Johnny dropped the stirrup and stared at Pa.

"And he's the only officer left here." Pa put his hand on Johnny's shoulder, giving him a hard look. "When you're out there, be wary. Trust your common sense.

Don't underestimate how desperate the Dakota are."

Johnny sprang up into the saddle, neck-reining his horse to the fort entrance. "Everyone will find that out soon enough."

AMBUSH

Midmorning, August 18, 1862

Shouting and gesturing, a crowd of civilians and soldiers milled around four wagons jostling into position near the fort entrance. Mules brayed, stomping up clouds of dust as teamsters double-checked their harnesses. A sweat-drenched sergeant, bearded though seemingly no older than Lieutenant Gere, herded his troops toward the wagon boxes. Johnny rode up beside a uniformed man mounted on a mule, glad to see someone older and hopefully wiser than the officers he had so far encountered. "Peter Quinn? I'm Johnny Preuss." Peter, dark-haired and dark-eyed, nodded and shook hands.

Sergeant Quinn, spotting Captain Marsh forging his mule through the crowd, yelled to his soldiers, "Form up! We're moving out!" The stragglers scrambled aboard, the sergeant directing ten to twelve men in a wagon.

"Company, forward!" Captain Marsh's command

boomed out over his troops. He kicked his mule in the ribs and led his detail out of Fort Ridgely. Johnny and Peter, the only others mounted, rode behind him. Mules braying, wagon wheels squealing, the train lumbered past people shouting good-bye and good luck. Johnny turned and waved to Pa and Ma and Amy, standing beside Eliza Mueller on her porch. Ma had one hand over her heart.

Dust and heat billowed up around the wagon train, and Johnny was glad he rode near its front. "I thought everyone would be mounted," he said to Peter, keeping his voice low so Marsh wouldn't overhear.

"The Union army down south has nearly all the horses. We've got mules and wagons. They get us where we need to be." Peter nodded ahead at Captain Marsh. "The captain's a good officer. He did well in the war. Fought at Bull Run."

"He fought in the War Between the States?" Johnny rubbed tightened muscles in his neck. "But did he ever fight Indians?"

Peter shrugged. "No. Sergeant Bishop has, though."

Johnny was sure they'd all get a chance today. As they crossed the wide prairie, he constantly surveyed the countryside. Everything looked peaceful. Hot dusty miles rolled away under the wagons. An hour passed. Then two. Tension squirmed back into Johnny's neck as he realized it felt *too* peaceful.

A rumbling cloud of dust surrounding a buckboard raced toward them. Bishop quickly waved his wagons to the edge of the road. The oncoming driver hauled back on the reins, managing to stop his team before he collided with the troop wagons. Johnny pulled his horse aside, recognizing the frantic driver—this time it was Reverend Hinman. His load of white-faced refugees grasped the sideboards as if to save their souls.

The black-frocked reverend rose up from the wagon seat like he was ascending his pulpit and began preaching at Captain Marsh. "The Indians are killing everyone at the Agency. Every trader, every clerk! Women and children, too! And every Indian and half-breed that cuts his hair and farms and wears white man's clothes. And comes to my church!" His plague-and-pestilence voice thundered across them all.

The reverend's arm shot out, aiming at Marsh. "Don't go to the Agency! You're outnumbered three to one." He whirled his whip over his team, cracking it like a rifle shot. The horses bolted and the wagon flew off down the road, the terrified people in it hanging on for dear life.

Marsh, Johnny, and Peter calmed their mounts; the teamsters struggled to get back in position. "Can't be but a handful," Marsh called back to Sergeant Bishop driving the troop wagon. "The chiefs don't want war. They'll find the marauders for us and bring them to the fort for justice." With his arm, he waved the troops forward.

Johnny stared openmouthed at Peter, wondering what it would take to convince Marsh this was deadly business.

Peter, grim-faced, nudged his mule in line behind the captain. "Captain gives the orders," he said.

Johnny followed too, his neck as tight as a bow-string. He was certain that Marsh was dead wrong, that danger lay ahead.

After the ruckus of Hinman's turbulent message, quiet settled again on the company and the countryside. No one spoke. No crows cawing, no grasshoppers scritch-scratching. Johnny thought Hinman must have scared every living creature off the face of the earth. Clip-clopping mules plodded on for several miles. Then suddenly, Marsh's mule slowed, its neck stretched out, long ears pointed forward. Marsh stopped, raising his hand to halt the wagon train. Sergeant Bishop jumped off the wagon seat and ran to him. Johnny's stomach tightened. He didn't like this.

"There're bodies lying in the road," said Marsh, pointing. Bishop ran ahead several yards and stooped over a man sprawled in the dirt. He rolled him over, then glanced on down the road. He dashed over to three more bodies, a woman and two little girls; hands all joined like the mother was keeping them together. "All dead," he yelled back. Marsh rode his mule closer.

Johnny stayed back, his eyes searching the tall weeds and grass rimming the dirt road. Thick raspberry canes and wild grapevines provided lots of cover. Was someone in there? Johnny ducked his head so his hat brim shaded his eyes. Spotting terrified blue eyes, he dismounted, knelt, and reached out his hand.

A half-grown boy bolted out of the brush straight into Johnny's arms. "It's my father! Indians chased us and shot at us. Father shoved me into the brush and told me to hide." A shudder ran through the youngster's body as he spotted not only his father, but also his mother and sisters, all dead in their tracks.

Johnny tightened his arms around the boy. "You're safe now."

Captain Marsh rode up. "What's your name, son?"

The boy looked up at the captain and blinked into bright sunlight. "I'm John Humphrey, but my father calls me Hans. We live at the Sioux Agency. My father's Philander Humphrey, the doctor there." He looked over at his family lying in the road and fell silent.

Captain Marsh turned to Sergeant Bishop. "Are there any shovels in the wagons? We haven't got time to take their bodies back to the fort."

"We haven't got time to bury them, either." Bishop stood, legs straddled over the doctor's body. "Not if those Indians are still rampaging around killing people."

Marsh nodded and glanced at the Humphrey boy. "We can't leave you here. You'll have to come with us."

"Ride with me," said Johnny. He led the young boy to his horse, mounted, and hoisted the boy up behind him. The boy's arms tightened around Johnny's waist, his face leaned into his shoulder, hiding his eyes. Bishop's men carried the bodies to the side of the road, and the wagon train moved on.

Marsh halted the company again at the edge of a bluff overlooking the river. Pillars of flames and smoke columns dotted the valley below. The captain sat rigid on his mule, silently taking in the scene, his lips tightly pursed. Soldiers stood in their wagons counting the fires.

Johnny rode up beside Captain Marsh. "Those are all settlers' cabins. The Indians seem to have wiped out the Agency settlement and fanned out through the countryside attacking homesteads."

Saying nothing, Marsh led his caravan down the winding dirt road into the valley. More corpses littered the roadway, like the Humphreys, families killed in flight. The troop stopped only long enough to move the bodies to the side of the road. Acrid black smoke stopped them again as they came upon a cabin engulfed by fire. Snarling flames consumed the logs that fell in on each other with a roar and a burst of cinders. A bad smell whooshed over Johnny, like animals had been caught in a barn fire. Marsh called again to Bishop. "See if there's anyone left alive, maybe hiding somewhere."

The sergeant stood up on his wagon seat, giving a cursory glance around the burning ruins. "No bodies in sight. I reckon the folks who lived here hid in the cabin. That'd account for the stink. There's no place to hide except in the brush. Don't think you want me to holler for 'em, do you?"

Johnny cringed, knowing they'd better be quiet. The boy behind him dug his fingers into Johnny's gut. "Safest place right now is with these soldiers," Johnny whispered to him, unsure that anyone was safe here at all.

Marsh shook his head and asked, "How far are we from the river landing?"

"About a mile," said Bishop.

"Leave the wagons here. Follow on foot. Keep it quiet." Bishop nodded. The troops slipped over the wagon boards and formed up quieter than Johnny could have imagined.

The sun neared high noon as they approached the river landing. The road led right to the river's edge, the brown water flowing rapidly, too deep to ford. A ferry-boat was tied to its mooring as though waiting for them to board. No ferryman about, though. Across the river, the narrow dirt road wound up through a heavily wooded ravine to the Agency settlement.

The company halted. Marsh looked around him. Hazel and willow thickets grew close to the road, long whippy branches dragging into the dirt.

Johnny pointed to tangled roadside brush, trampled and hummocky. "Better check that out, Captain. Something disturbed those bushes."

Sergeant Bishop ran into the tall river grass, parting the rushes. "Lord Almighty! It's Charlie the ferryman! Hacked to pieces!" He stumbled backward onto the road. No one ran up for a closer look.

Johnny's eyes searched the dense overhanging brush. It was too quiet. Always there should be red-winged blackbirds around the river. He glanced left—a high sandbank cut off any view south. It was way too quiet.

"Soldiers!" Across the river, an Indian stepped into view and pointed to the ferry. "Come over. Parlay with us." Peter rode forward and translated.

"Who's that?" Marsh asked. "What's he saying?"

Johnny eased up beside them. "That's White Dog. He used to work at the Agency, but Galbraith told him to leave. He wanted to hire his own men. I wouldn't trust him."

White Dog called again across the water, beckoning them to come. "The trouble's over. Come and parlay in our village," Peter translated.

Marsh shifted in his saddle, apparently undecided. "Don't trust him!" Johnny hissed.

Sergeant Bishop ran up to the captain, grasping the skittish mule's bridle. "Two of my men saw Indians hiding in the brush on the other side of the river. And there're Indian ponies over this sand hill. Nothing's over yet!"

Marsh's mule pawed the ground. Johnny's horse shook its head, prancing sideways. Marsh told Peter, "Ask White Dog why there's so many ponies here if everyone's at the village."

Peter stared aghast at the captain. "You expect him to tell us if Indians are hiding in the brush?"

"Do it!" Marsh repeated.

Peter shot a disgusted look at Johnny, then called the question over to White Dog. Immediately, dozens of bullets slammed into Peter, jerking him backward, sideways. He pitched forward and fell with a thud to the ground. Gunfire ripped into the troops from all directions. Johnny slid to the ground, pulling the Humphrey boy with him. Gunshots, yells, and screams clamored as soldiers scrambled for cover.

Marsh's mule was shot out from under him, but Marsh jumped free. "Return fire!" he yelled, shooting behind him. "They've taken the ferry house!" His troops rallied around him and fired a volley, wholly exposed. Within seconds, a dozen soldiers lay dead in the road. Johnny dashed into the brush, dragging the boy by the wrist, heading for the denser woods. He heard Marsh order a retreat, and the surviving soldiers scattered into the brush all around Johnny. Farther and deeper into the thicket they ran, stumbling, shoving through brush that snagged and tore at them.

Finally, deep into the thicket, the gunshots and yells receded. His heart thudding fiercely, Johnny collapsed to the ground, the boy beside him. Marsh and Bishop took cover beneath a large willow. The others scattered nearby. Everyone listened. Even the trees quieted. No sounds except the rush of the river and the wind softly rustling the slender willow branches. It seemed the Indians had not pursued them into the woods.

The survivors, about twenty of them, some wounded and bleeding, gathered themselves around Marsh and Bishop. Johnny and the boy crept over there, too. The willow drooped its covering branches down around them as if weeping over them. Everyone slowly regained steady breath and wits.

"Why aren't they coming after us?" whispered young Humphrey, leaning against Johnny. Everyone looked at them, obviously wondering the same thing.

Johnny reached his arm around Hans's shoulder. "They're waiting till we come out of the woods."

"Can't we just stay here?" Hans looked as if he never wanted to leave.

"No. We'll have to leave before they get tired of waiting and come in after us." Johnny shot a determined look at Marsh.

"You live near here, don't you? You know this area." Marsh's tone was still commanding. "Guide us out. I'm thinking we've got no time to waste."

Johnny stood, telling himself he could do this, that scouting must be akin to hunting. He realized that the breeze was southerly. The whooshing rush of the river also came from the south. "This thicket's about two miles long, and we're likely surrounded on all sides but the river. The Indians have the crossing guarded, but we might find an isolated bend where we could ford the river or swim across and make our way back to the fort along the south shore."

Through thorny raspberry canes and over rotted

deadfalls, Johnny led them. The stifling heat was near to smothering them; the mosquitoes were a torment. Reaching the riverbank, they stopped to smear mud on their hands, faces, and necks.

"There's a sharp bend here," noted Captain Marsh. "It's out of sight of the Indians."

Johnny looked upstream and down. It seemed well-protected, but the river rushed fast and furious around the bends and channeled through high banks.

"I'll go first," said Marsh. "It looks deep—we may have to swim." He waded out into the water, holding his rifle high to keep it dry. With every step, he went deeper. Soon he was swimming, holding the rifle aloft with one hand and stroking with the other. Suddenly he grimaced, dropped his rifle, and clutched his leg.

A cramp! thought Johnny. It's near to crippling him; he won't make it.

Almost immediately Marsh went underwater, coming up several yards downstream. He did not call out. Two of his men dove in after him, struggling to get to him. Marsh's head and arm poked up once more, then he was sucked down into a swirling whirlpool. He never came up. His would-be rescuers struggled ashore downstream and returned dripping wet and shivering.

Stunned silent, Johnny, the Humphrey boy, and the surviving men crouched under an overhanging riverbank. Johnny shivered in spite of the hot day. What could he do now?

Sergeant Bishop grasped Johnny's arm. "Johnny, you take my corporal and young Humphrey and half of the men. We'll have a better chance if we separate. Try crossing farther south." He gathered his wounded. "I'll take these men."

It made sense. "Meet you back at the fort," said Johnny, glad to have direction.

Trudging through slippery mud and wet rocks, struggling to stay under the riverbank's overhang, they made their way southeast. Around the next bend, the river widened and Johnny could see that a sandbank glinted just under the surface. Cautiously, he waded into the river, wary of drop-offs. Water tugged at his legs. Sand shifted under his feet. Johnny watched for whirls and eddies, avoiding them. Step after step, going deeper each time, but the water was never more than chest-deep. Climbing out on the opposite bank, he waved the others to follow his route. Finally, everyone emerged and scrambled up the bank into the tangled brush.

Johnny motioned for them to sit and rest as he quickly scouted the area. A path carved a narrow trail parallel to the river. Johnny knelt beside it, searching for signs of recent use. He saw nothing but deer tracks.

Old deer tracks. Neither deer nor men had used the path in a long time. It headed in the direction of the fort—a chance to get back undetected.

The sun settled itself lower in the sky, and an evening breeze made Johnny shiver in his wet clothes. But the cold wasn't all that made him shiver. A long perilous trek lay ahead, and he would be the hunted, not the hunter. Johnny wished Chaska were there to help him. Chaska would know where to go, would know how to get everyone back safely. Chaska would . . . Where was Chaska now?

Johnny realized he had to do this alone. He had to begin by not thinking of himself as prey. He had to protect these men. "Follow close," he whispered, beckoning Hans and the half dozen soldiers with him. "And for God's sake, don't make any noise."

Frightened faces stared at Johnny, nodded at his words. The Humphrey boy gripped his hand tightly, as if it were his link between life and death.

Sniffing the breeze, alert for unnatural sounds, glancing from path to brush to treetops, Johnny led his charges home.

WHERE LIES THE GLORY?

Evening, August 18, 1862

After giving a brief report to Lieutenant Gere and a fuller account to his father, Johnny made his way through the evening to the stables. He needed a saddle horse to find Chaska, no matter how risky sneaking out of the fort might be. He was worried sick about Chaska and his parents. Johnny knew he'd not sleep tonight until he could talk to his friend.

The sentry on duty at the stables recognized Johnny and motioned him inside. Johnny shook a groom sleeping on a haymow. "Any chance of getting a mount to go scouting?"

The groom bolted up, brushed at bits of straw in his hair and clothes. "No chance at all—too few animals left as it is. Besides, you'd need permission from the commanding officer, whoever that is now. Lieutenant Sheehan back yet?"

"Not that I've heard." Johnny walked down the aisle between the tie stalls. "What's behind those hay bundles?" Concealed in shadows, a large stagecoach loomed over nearby wagons and buggies. "Was a stage attacked?"

"It's the stage from St. Paul. Arrived about noon. It brought the Indians' annuity payment. Seventy-one thousand in gold!"

Johnny's jaw dropped. "The gold payment? It came today?"

"Yup. Too late to do any good. Lieutenant Gere put it in the commissary cellar."

"Danged government!" Johnny spit out between clenched teeth. "If that payment had been on time, there wouldn't have been any killings."

The groom shrugged. "The guard said everything was delayed because of the war in the South. Troops need food and uniforms and medicine, guns and cannons and ammunition, horses and mules. It all costs. The guard said the government would bankrupt itself trying to keep the Union together. He was surprised anything for the Indians had come through at all."

Johnny turned abruptly and strode back down the aisle behind the horses, clenching and unclenching his fists. He needed to find Chaska. "The settlers brought their animals with them. I wouldn't take an army mule, but how about lending me a farm horse? Just for an hour."

~~~

Johnny cantered away softly on a small but sturdy Morgan horse, riding bareback, staying to the soft edge of the road. After a few miles, he pulled up under a large spreading maple whose branches lent a thicker darkness to the night. Watching the nearby fork in the road, he stroked his horse's neck to keep him from getting restless. He hoped Chaska would remember this place. Little knots twisted in Johnny's stomach. What if Chaska had joined the braves in the fighting? What if Chaska wanted to drive the whites off the land that had long belonged to the Dakota? How could Johnny even ask him about it?

Small normal night sounds resumed. Frogs sang in a nearby bog. A slight cool breeze, smelling of swamp, ruffled Johnny's hair. He rubbed the horse's neck, his fingers working out tangles in the mane. He listened, and he waited. Occasionally Johnny would imitate a mourning dove's call, his hunting signal. The horse's head gradually hung down.

Johnny called the mourning doves again. If Chaska didn't come soon, he'd have to return to the fort.

Just then, Johnny heard a fox's peculiar bark. He sat upright, dove-calling again. Chaska responded, nearer this time. Call and call again, fox and dove, till Chaska appeared on his pony. They clasped hands above the wrists.

"Is your family safe? whispered Chaska.

"Yes, at the fort. And yours?"

"We were at the Upper Agency. A large group of settlers had gathered in a stone warehouse. My father will take them and my mother north, perhaps as far as St. Paul. I came to tell you that my father thinks Little Crow will attack Fort Ridgely tomorrow."

"Little Crow has enough braves to attack the fort?" The knots in Johnny's stomach twisted tighter.

"With no troops left to oppose them, the Dakota could reclaim land all the way to St. Paul." Chaska's voice stayed quiet, neutral.

Johnny kneaded his knotted abdomen with his hand. The fort would be overwhelmed. All the people there would be killed.

"But remember, the braves have been killing settlers, taking horses and goods and prisoners." A trace of anger crept into Chaska's voice. "They may not listen to Little Crow, they will go their own way and do what they want. Attacking more settlements, perhaps towns."

"What about you?" Having finally asked the question, the words cascaded out of Johnny's mind and mouth. "Your heart is with the Dakota—I've seen it."

"The only thing I know now is that I could never harm the people I love or let anyone else harm them." Chaska's voice steadied. "That's another reason I came back—to make sure Star Woman and Raven are protected. Little Crow's village must be in an uproar, and . . ."

Hair prickled up on the back of Johnny's neck. Suddenly galloping hoofbeats stormed in like thunderclouds. Billowing black shapes engulfed them. A spectral horse, dark as the threatening night, crowded up against Johnny. Like lightning, a rough hand flashed out and snatched the reins from Johnny's grasp.

Warriors! The realization slammed Johnny like a war club.

With a harsh grunt, the brave whirled the Morgan horse around, kicking it in the ribs, jerking hard on the reins. Johnny clamped his knees around his horse's ribs and clutched desperately at the whipping mane. Swept away with the war party, his thoughts raced like the stampeding horses. *Why were they being taken captive? Would they be tortured for information? Scalped alive?*

The horses, hell-bent on a dead run, jostled and crowded and shoved each other, snorting for air. Lather and sweat splattered off them. Mile after mile, they careened blindly through thick woods, narrowly avoiding the branches and limbs that could snatch the riders off their horses. Careening down steep ravines, they plunged into rushing creeks and scrambled through mud and sand and rocks. Finally, Johnny saw firelight ahead from many campfires—Little Crow's village.

Screaming triumphant war cries, the warriors raced through the rows of teepees, scattering people and dogs and tethered horses every which way. At the end of the village, with one whoop they turned and trotted back, reining up the spent horses at the largest campfire, in front of the largest teepee. The Warrior's Lodge.

His captor dragged Johnny off his horse and forced him to his knees in front of the snarling fire. His rough hand squeezed Johnny's shoulder like a plank in a vise. A knifepoint jabbed the back of Johnny's neck, and he froze, turning only his eyes as Chaska was pushed down beside him.

Chaska took a deep quiet breath and let it out, blinked his eyes slowly, almost lazily. Johnny took the cue. He should be calm and silent, show no fear.

Yells and thumping drumbeats summoned the villagers to the Warrior's Lodge. Moving eyes only, Johnny surveyed the encampment. There was a lot of celebrating going on. Many farm wagons were scattered throughout, haphazardly piled with all kinds of stuff. Every teepee had a cook pot stewing over its campfire, every woman cooking suddenly plentiful food. There were lots of horses, lots of guns, lots of liquor, and lots of captives.

Between the whoops and hollers of celebrating warriors, Johnny discerned crying children and moaning women. He wasn't the only captive. From every direction came the sounds of slaps and angry commanding yells. Is this what Chaska meant by "uproar"?

Shouting braves swarmed around the Warrior's Lodge, eager to see what the war party had brought back. Firelight danced over their faces, cavorted over their painted, bloodied bodies. Sweat and grease running down their chests, the exultant warriors celebrated victory and revenge.

Sharp stones cut into Johnny's knees, but he dared not shift his weight. His head pounded, though he wasn't sure if it was from drumbeats or his own heartbeat. He took long deep breaths, telling himself take it easy, be like Chaska.

A pathway parted the throng of warriors as a stone-faced Little Crow strode up to the fire, eagle feathers cascading down his back. War drums crescendoed to a deafening roar, then silenced abruptly. The braves stepped back and Chief Little Crow thundered, "Who are these captives? Why a brave with a white man?"

Johnny's head was jerked back by the hair and the knife blade pressed across his forehead. "This scalp is mine! And I would have an eagle feather with it!" the warrior holding Johnny demanded.

Little Crow did not respond. He focused on Chaska. "This is a brave I have seen before, at the Warrior's Lodge. Why is he held captive?"

"I am Chaska, son of Other Day," Chaska said before anyone else could speak, his voice deep, authoritative. "I was speaking with my white friend, telling him to flee, to leave the territory to the Dakota." His eyes lifted to Little Crow. "Nearly everyone here has a white friend he would save. Even Little Crow has friends and relatives among the whites." His challenging gaze did not leave Little Crow's face.

Johnny expected a knife in both their throats within seconds. The blood pounded louder in his head and ears. He didn't move a muscle, didn't take any more deep breaths. The fire crackled and snapped. The flames flared and snarled, spitting out coals and embers.

A shadowy figure entered the circle and stood beside Little Crow. Dressed in fringed leather, hawk feathers in her braids, her old face was as regal as the chief's— Star Woman! Johnny forced himself to be still and silent.

She glared at the encircling warriors, but her words struck Little Crow. "This warrior is Chaska, son of Other Day and grandson of Star Woman!"

No one spoke, not even Little Crow. Star Woman continued. "Little Crow seeks allies with the Dakota at the Upper Agency and with the Sisseton. Would you make enemies of them by killing the son of Other Day? And the white boy has always been a friend to us; he brings us food and blankets. He also is under the protection of Other Day."

Little Crow stared at Chaska and Johnny for a very long moment. His voice boomed across the village like war drums. "Warriors! Tomorrow the deciding battles begin! You've killed soldiers in battle and won eagle feathers and glory for yourselves. You've also killed women and children, but there is no honor in their killing. I will award no eagle feathers for such actions!"

Muttering broke out among a group of braves nearby. Little Crow's stern order silenced them. "Stop drinking the white man's liquor. Forget looting and taking captives. Prepare yourself for war with a worthy enemy. Tomorrow we ride against Fort Ridgely!"

His arm swept toward Chaska and Johnny, his voice fearless and commanding. "Release the white boy. He is of no consequence." His attention turned to Chaska. "Come to my house. I would speak with you." Little Crow turned and disappeared through the crowd of warriors. Chaska's captor released him with a shove and a snarl. Chaska staggered a few steps, then trotted after

Little Crow without a backward glance.

The grip on Johnny's hair tightened, pulling his head farther back, exposing his throat. Star Woman stepped up to the warrior holding Johnny. Her black eyes reflected flames as she glared at the furious warrior. At her signal, Raven brought up Johnny's horse.

"I would have his horse!" the warrior spat out. "I captured it!"

"You have captured more horses than you can care for." Star Woman's voice was as steely as the warrior's knife. "Mark it with your war paint to show your bravery in its capture. Carve a notch in your coup stick. Then let them go."

Johnny's head was jerked farther back; he felt the razor-sharp blade draw down the side of his face tracing his jawline, felt blood trickling down his neck. He gasped, not yet feeling pain. A kick in the small of his back sent Johnny sprawling into the dirt, his head slammed down close to the hot stones of the fire ring that spat cinders in his face. He jumped quickly to his feet, fighting off dizziness.

The warrior wiped the blood off his knife onto the horse's neck, giving the bridle a vicious jerk as the horse shied away. "Now they are both marked," growled the warrior. He strode briskly into the Warrior's Lodge.

Johnny leaped onto the skittish horse, struggling

against nausea. Drops of blood splattered onto Raven's arm as Johnny leaned down for the reins. He winced as the sudden movement stung his face and pulled at the piercing cut.

Raven paid no notice. "Chaska says, 'Warn New Ulm,'" she muttered, stepping back into shadows before Johnny could respond. Star Woman had already disappeared.

Whirling his horse, Johnny raced out of Little Crow's village like an arrow shot from a bow.

WARN NEW ULM
Early Tuesday, August 19, 1862

Johnny leaned against the galloping horse's neck, its mane whipping against his throbbing jaw. Nearly prone on the Morgan's back, knees gripping fiercely, he urged it to run faster. The horse's neck flattened out, its gait lengthened as if knowing lives depended on its speed. Johnny's thoughts flew just as wildly in the dark night. What if Little Crow prevailed, first attacking Fort Ridgely? If so, instead of riding to warn New Ulm, shouldn't he be going to the fort?

Galloping hooves beneath him thudded in rhythm with his racing mind. Warn Fort Ridgely. Warn New Ulm. Warn Fort Ridgely. Warn New Ulm. He nearly turned back toward Fort Ridgely, toward Ma, Pa, and Amy, but didn't. Unchecked, the horse raced steadily on to New Ulm, sure-footed through the night, as if knowing better than his rider where to go. Johnny didn't turn him. Fort Ridgely was aware of what was coming; New Ulm wasn't.

Not discerning space or time, unaware of the whipping wind and biting pain in his face, Johnny sped through clutching darkness until he saw lights. Steady lights, not flickering, not campfires. They were lanterns, on streets and in windows. Thank God, New Ulm was still safe. He pulled his horse in slightly, slowing to a canter, then a trot.

New Ulm bustled with activity. Hundreds of people milled anxiously about in the streets, all talking and gesturing and arguing. Johnny didn't understand much of what they said—most of it was in German—but he was sure it was about the attacks. Refugees had flocked to New Ulm as well as to Fort Ridgely.

Johnny dismounted at Sheriff Roos's office and called a couple of boys over. He told them to walk his horse slow, let it cool down before giving it water. Staring open-mouthed from Johnny's bloody face to the heaving horse, they took the reins and walked off without question. Inside the sheriff's office, lamplight silhouetted two standing men, apparently in serious discussion. Johnny entered without knocking.

The broad and bulky sheriff looked over, startled. He walked up to Johnny, took hold of his chin, and turned his face to one side. "Aren't you Henry Preuss's son? You're all blood! What happened to your face?"

The other man, young and strong with a big handlebar mustache, stepped in close. "Indians do that? Did they attack your farm? Is your family all right?"

Stepping back and away, Johnny put his hand to his cheek. He touched sticky clotted blood there, all the way down the side of his face. "Doesn't hurt anymore." He wiped his hand against his pants. "My family's safe at Fort Ridgely. But you're not. New Ulm will be attacked tomorrow."

"Tomorrow? How do you know about an attack on New Ulm?" The sheriff still focused on Johnny's bloody jaw.

"I had a run-in with some braves but got away. I heard them arguing about whether to attack New Ulm or Fort Ridgely." Johnny glanced nervously at their doubtful faces. Would these men believe him or react like Captain Marsh?

"I'm Jacob Nix," said the second man, his voice dead serious. "Lots of folks are flocking here, fleeing from Indians who are attacking homesteads. You're saying the towns will be next?"

Johnny nodded. "That's what I heard."

"It makes sense," said Jacob, giving the sheriff an 'I told you so' look. "Their best time to attack is when everyone's confused and unprepared."

"Then we'd better *get* prepared." The sheriff flung his arm toward the door. "Go organize those farmers and townsfolk into fighting squads. Set up defenses. Post sentries." Jacob charged out past him and clanged a dinner gong. The sheriff yelled out at a deputy. "George! Send runners to St. Peter for help—to William Dodd and Judge Flandreau." He looked back at Johnny. "You got a rifle?"

"Not with me, but I'm a good shot, if you've got an extra gun."

"First get yourself over to Dr. Weschcke at the Erd House. You look half-scalped; I don't want you scaring the womenfolk." Head still out the door, he pointed down the street. "He's been stitching up lots of folks today."

Johnny trotted toward the doctor's office. Already, Jacob had groups of men pulling buckboards, hay wagons, and buggies down the streets. They tipped and piled them to make barricades separating downtown from the houses scattered along the terraced river's edge. Women and children rushed into a big hotel called the Dakota House. As settlers streamed in from the countryside, their wagons soon emptied and became part of the barricades. New Ulm took things seriously, Johnny was glad to see. It steadied him some.

Dr. Weschcke flickered nary an eyelash at the sight of Johnny's face, just washed it and daubed it with alcohol. Johnny flinched when he felt sharp pricks and tugs on his cheek and closed his eyes. It was hard to open them again; he was so tired.

"When's the last time you slept?"

Johnny had to concentrate. Last night? No, he'd waited in the barn for Chaska and then gone to Fort Ridgely. Was it the night before? It seemed longer ago than that.

The doctor ushered him into a back room and pointed to a cot. "It's just past midnight. You'll be worth more tomorrow if you get a few hours' sleep." Fatigue slurred his own words.

Johnny sat on the taut canvas cot, pulled off his boots, lay back, and stretched out full length. Flickering lights from the lanterns outside crept in through the wavy window glass and scampered up and down the walls. They danced like the big campfire in Little Crow's village. He shut his eyes. What had happened to Chaska?

~~~

"Johnny, sun's coming up. Jump to it. Every able-bodied man needs to be on duty." Dr. Weschcke called in, then left immediately. Johnny flew off the cot and sat right back down, dizzy.

The doctor's wife bustled in with coffee and warm bread, her cheeks flushed from a hot cookstove. "Gut morning! Sit while I fix your face." She set the small tray on Johnny's lap and swabbed none-too-gently at his wound. Johnny squirmed sideways, grabbing the fresh warm bread. It smelled so good.

"Und sit still!" said Mrs. Weschcke, pulling aside his collar and scrubbing his neck. "There, now. Eat. Gut food und gut drink hold body and soul together, yah?"

After a hasty gulp and gobble, Johnny found Jacob Nix down the street supervising brewery workers stacking beer barrels across an intersection, constructing battle defenses. Tension crept back into his stomach, and the warm bread didn't sit so well anymore. "Anything happen overnight?" he asked Jacob.

"Just what you see." Jacob positioned Johnny at a piled-wagon barricade on Third Street and handed him an old rifle. "This belonged to a farmer who got killed by Indians. His widow gave it to me and told me to put it to good use." He pointed out a gap between the upended wagons to sight through. "Be careful who you shoot at. We sent out rescue parties at dawn to bring back farmers who might not know of the attacks until too late. They'll be coming in soon, I hope." He craned his neck over the top of the wagon pile, looking for them. "Have any idea when the Indians might attack? Hear anything about that?"

"I wouldn't expect them too early. They might go after Fort Ridgely first."

Jacob's eyes narrowed. He paced the barricaded roadway, yelling at people to look sharp, peering over the jumbled barricades again and again.

Sudden hooting laughter startled Johnny, and he jerked his head around. Who on God's green earth had anything to laugh about?

It came from the Dakota House. Great white sheets sailed off the balcony, fluttering like clouds shot out of the sky. Small boys scampered under them, letting them flip and fall over their heads, laughing till they hiccuped. Johnny looked closely. Were those round sheets?

"Hoopskirts," Jacob said, watching beside him. "Only so much room up there for ladies in hoopskirts. They must have decided they'd be more comfortable without."

Johnny smiled slightly at the boys' antics. Didn't do a body any good to get all scared and nervous, Ma always said. Johnny settled into his niche behind the wagon. But Ma and Pa would be nervous as all get out when they realized he wasn't at the fort. Ma'd be upset and Pa'd be downright mad. Sitting sideways to the boards, he glanced back into the town. What was going on down the street? Folks were running out of buildings and pulling away the barricade wagons. Whatever for? He ran closer, along the boardwalk. Through the widening gap, he saw a buckboard coming in at a reckless gallop. The driver was whipping the horses like all the demons in hell were chasing him. Everyone yelled and dashed out of the way.

Settlers outrunning Indians, Johnny thought. He had to jump lively as the wagon careened in through the opened gap. The horses, jerked up quickly, reared and bolted as onlookers ran to grab their bridles and harnesses. Caught in the gathering crowd, Johnny caught a glimpse of people riding in the back. He edged ahead. Three or four men were gripping the side rails. Arrows were stuck into the boards. The frantic passengers leapt out; the crowd all but carried them into the hotel.

A cold shiver raced through Johnny—the Dakota were ransacking the entire countryside. What might be happening at Fort Ridgely? Just as many settlers would be streaming in there. Had Sheehan's troops arrived back to defend the fort? He hoped to God Ma and Pa and Amy were safe. And he hoped he'd get back there tonight. He ran back to his post by the wagon-barricade.

And what of Chaska? Would Little Crow protect him? Or kill him as a traitor? Shaking his head, Johnny looked back out across the prairie. It'd be best to keep his mind on things he could do something about.

As the day wore on, the sun beat down hot. The air

got muggy, thick, and hard to breathe. Wrens sang from a nearby mock-orange bush. How odd that seemed: the sweet smell of mock-orange blossoms, the lovely trill of the wrens. The prairie grasses waved and billowed, the same as every day.

Johnny discerned no sign of Indians. He heard no distant gunfire and saw no smoke off to the north. Had they gone to Fort Ridgely after all? The sun climbed steadily overhead. Noon arrived. Someone brought bread and sausage and coffee around. The long, hot, sultry hours dragged by, piling up heavy on them all.

"Indians! On the bluffs!"

"Indians! Down by the river!"

From the surrounding hills and terraces and river-banks and prairie, gunfire pelted the town, targeting every flimsy fortification. Heart thudding, Johnny shoved his gun barrel through a gap in the wagon boards and sighted and fired. He jerked it back and jammed powder and shot down the barrel. Again, he shoved the gun through the gap, sighted, and fired. Indians were everywhere out there.

They were intent on taking the town, Johnny thought. They'd had no opposition when raiding homesteads, and ambushed the troops at the ferry with no trouble. He guessed they wouldn't stop at New Ulm. Not unless New Ulm stopped them. He shot again and again, not knowing if he hit anyone. Shots fired all around him—constant cracking gunshots. Acrid gun smoke layered the air, smarting his eyes, and making him cough. Settle down, settle down, he told himself. Sight and shoot.

Before long, the battle settled into a steady exchange of gunfire. Jacob called out orders. Sentries on rooftops yelled down sightings. No one seemed so panicky anymore.

Jacob ran up and sat beside Johnny as he reloaded. "Have you noticed? The Indians' firing isn't coordinated. Coming from everywhere, but it's like no one's in charge. Do you recognize any chiefs out there directing their attack?"

"You're right; it seems random." Johnny quickly surveyed the landscape. "I don't see any chiefs. The braves must be acting alone."

"Soldiers without officers—hah! That will be their undoing." Jacob stuck his rifle through a gap and fired. "Hey, there're Indians in that small house just outside the barricade." He turned and yelled down the street. "Daniel! Take some men and get the Kiesling house back. Burn it if you have to."

A group of men dashed through a building, bursting out onto the exposed street beyond the barricade. They fired steadily into a framed cabin, breaking windows, peppering it with bullets. Indians streamed out the back door and windows as Daniel's men kicked through the front entrance. Black powder smoke hung low and heavy, but Johnny saw the Indians were on the run.

Wiping his sweaty palms on his shirt, Johnny sighted his rifle again, covering Daniel and his men as they hastened back inside the barricaded area. He sat to reload, glancing down Center Street. It was empty now—everyone was inside buildings or at barricades. No, wait. Johnny saw someone in a doorway, looking out. Bright plaid skirts flashed as a girl with blonde braids dashed across the dusty street.

"Stay back!" Johnny yelled. At that same instant, a shot fired from the hillside. The girl pitched facedown. Dust whirled up where she fell, and her skirts billowed down softly around her. Her braids slid into the dirt. Blood spread out beneath her in creeping red rivulets.

Johnny couldn't move. He should run to her, but he couldn't breathe. Darkness crept around the edges of his eyesight. He should go to her. Someone near him fired a shot. "Got him!" Johnny dimly heard. Johnny staggered up and lurched forward a step. Jacob grabbed his shirtsleeve and pulled him back.

Two men dashed out of the hotel, grabbed the girl under her shoulders and knees, and scurried back inside. Johnny stared at the puddled blood, thinking about how that girl could have been Amy—that that girl was *someone's* Amy. Everything got blurry, dark. Someone whacked him on the back, then shook him. Johnny struggled to think—where was he? Jacob whacked him again, shouting his name.

A sudden thunderous rumble split the air, shaking buildings and rattling windows. Dazed, Johnny looked around him. Everything was still so dark. He looked up. Huge roiling black clouds swept toward them like a vengeful sky attacking the earth. Sudden great gusts of wind whooshed through, sucking up dusty whirlwinds. Another great rumble roared.

Thunder. It was thunder. A tremendous thunder-storm bore down on them, fast and furious. Lightning slashed at treetops, church spires, rocky outcrops. Continuous angry thunderclaps ripped the sky, drowning out all sounds of gunfire. Sheets of gray icy rain pelted the town, the prairie, and the wooded hills. The Indians scattered.

"They're leaving!" called a drenched sentry from the rooftop.

Johnny hunkered under the wagon; cold wet rain poured through his hair and down his neck, bringing him back to reality. He realized he was in New Ulm, and the battle was over. Men ran past him and pulled away the Center Street barricade.

Why? thought Johnny. Surely there would be no more refugees. Who would dare come through a battle? A buggy and several horsemen careened into the street, splashing mud, and slid to a stop. Johnny joined the crowd running to the splattered buggy.

A huge dripping-wet gentleman dashed into the scant shelter afforded by the Dakota House verandah, the dismounting riders close behind him. "Boardman's the name. From St. Peter." He raised soggy eyebrows as he looked over the bedraggled defenders: rainwater pouring off felt hats, smears of mud on coats, wet caked dirt on faces. "Looks like we came just in time. We sure scared off those Indians!"

Angry hoots and hollers erupted from the crowd. Sheriff Roos shouted, "The brave men here and God's timely thunderstorm won this battle, no thanks to you!" But he quickly added, "Glad you're here, though. We'll need all the help we can get."

Jacob stepped onto the Dakota. "Any more reinforcements coming?" he asked Boardman.

Boardman looked like he would like to continue the argument over who saved this battle, but he had news to deliver. "Judge Flandreau's bringing our Frontier Guards, mostly St. Peter and LeSueur residents. I expect they'll be here before nightfall, if the storm doesn't hold them up. And he's bringing Dr. Mayo and

Dr. Daniels." He brushed his wet coat sleeves. "We sent to Mankato for help, too. Towns all around are full of refugees. Houses and churches jammed, streets full of farm animals. One big noisy mess." He stomped his boots to dislodge mud.

"Any news from Fort Ridgley?" Johnny asked.

Boardman wiped the rain from his face and hair with a big rumpled handkerchief. "Tom Galbraith took his Renville Rangers there. A volunteer regiment he's been training to send to the war in the South. A bunch of half-breeds, but they can shoot."

Johnny turned to Jacob Nix. "I'm heading back to Fort Ridgley."

Jacob nodded. "Take the Redstone ferry to the north side of the river." He shook Johnny's hand. "Godspeed."

Johnny jumped over the porch railing, avoiding a mud puddle. A flash of lightning lit his way to the livery stable.

SETTLERS' REFUGE

Evening, August 19, 1862

Chased by a brisk breeze, the still-rumbling storm clouds reluctantly fled the setting sun. Johnny's long loping shadow cantered ahead of him as he approached Fort Ridgely. Everything looked peaceful, normal. He wiped his still-wet sleeve across his face, wincing as the rough fabric brushed his cheek. His heart slowed. Again, he thanked God.

Johnny trotted around back to the stable and dismounted. No one around. Everyone must still be at mess. Horses, oxen, and cattle crowded together in the corral, all bellowing and shoving toward a small manger filled with fresh meadow hay. With a loud bawl and a few head butts, Bessie had gotten herself in front of the herd. She glared at Johnny as she snatched a mouthful of sweet clover. Nothing unusual here.

Johnny led the Morgan to its tie stall, brushed it down, and poured a measure of oats into the feed box. All the other animals had been fed; evening chores had been attended to. Johnny walked across the stretch of meadow that separated the log stable from Headquarters. He had to find Pa straightaway and let him know he was back safe. He rubbed his hands dry on his pants leg. He ought not to have left without telling his father. Pa was gonna be steaming mad and boiling over.

Johnny glimpsed lots of folks bustling about inside the fort. Cannon crews were swabbing out the gun barrels. Soldiers were oiling down their rifles, drilling and marching. Settlers hastily barricaded the gaps between the buildings, just as the New Ulm citizens had done. Wooden boxes, barrels, and sacks of flour formed a sturdy wall from Headquarters to the Officers' Quarters, with a twelve-pound cannon positioned in its center. Everyone was busy. Johnny felt a body could walk right in without drawing any attention. "Hello, inside!" he yelled.

A startled bearded face topped with a sergeant's cap popped up over the huge gun barrel. "Who's there?"

"Sergeant Bishop! You got yourself back from the Redwood ferry?" A grin spread across Johnny's face, stretching his scab. He yelped, quickly scrambling under and through the caisson wheels.

"Johnny! Where in tarnation have you been?" The sergeant motioned to one of his gun crew. "Get Henry

Preuss. Tell him his son is here." He thumped Johnny on the back. "Your Pa's none too happy with you. Your Ma neither."

"I wasn't gone intentionally, leastwise not for so long. Ended up in New Ulm."

"New Ulm? Best you report to Lieutenant Sheehan then. . . ." As the sergeant spoke, a stern young man with lieutenant bars on his collar strode toward them, Pa but a few steps behind. Lieutenant Sheehan, tall and straight as an ironwood tree, stopped a few inches from Johnny's face. His black beard was neat and trim. Johnny swallowed. He darted a glance at Pa, standing right alongside, hands on his hips and a big scowl on his face.

"You were at New Ulm? What's their situation?" The lieutenant's deep voice demanded an immediate response.

Johnny cleared his throat. "Crowded with refugees. But we withstood an Indian attack this afternoon. An uncoordinated attack, only braves." He sneaked a glance at Pa. Pa's eyebrows furrowed over a deep frown. "Reinforcements from St. Peter arrived just before I left. More are on the way. They expect another assault." Johnny's gaze swept the parade ground.

"There's no sentry at your stables," Johnny added. "I walked right on through them, across the meadow, and into the fort."

"What!" barked the lieutenant. Abruptly he turned and yelled at a nearby sergeant and shouted orders, pointing at the Headquarters rooftop, which overlooked the stable meadow. Turning to Pa, Sheehan said, "The stable is too isolated. Can you get corrals and pickets set up in the parade ground? Move the settlers' animals inside?" He noticed Pa's steady glare at Johnny. "I'll leave it in your hands." He strode back into Headquarters.

Pa got right in Johnny's face. "Thank the good Lord you're alive and well!" Pa's voice was like a demand from God himself. "Don't you *ever* leave without telling me!"

Johnny swallowed hard. "Yes, Pa. No, Pa. I promise. . . ."

"Johnny! Johnny!" Ma pushed through throngs of refugees and flung her arms around Johnny. She grabbed him and hugged him, crying and clutching. He hugged back. Amy wrapped her arms around both of them.

"Ma, I'm so sorry. I expected I'd be right back." Johnny wiped his own eyes. He should have known how dangerous his trip was. How easily he could have been killed. But now it was over and he was back. For sure and certain, he'd never leave again without telling anyone. He patted Ma's back as her crying softened.

Pa stretched his arm around Johnny's shoulder and tugged him loose. "There's lots that needs doing," he said, his voice gruff and scratchy. "And not much time to do it."

Ma reached over and touched Johnny's jagged scab. Her other hand went over her mouth with a sharp intake of breath. Amy's eyes widened.

"Just a nasty scratch. The doctor in New Ulm fixed it up." Johnny kissed Ma and Amy. "I have to go with Pa now." He followed Pa toward a cluster of farmers near the commissary.

"Elmer," called Pa. "Clarence, you too." He summoned a group around him. "Get your shovels and tools. We're going to build a corral inside the fort for our animals. It might not be safe to leave them in the stables." He pointed at a nearby stack of hitching rails. "We can use these for fencing. Anyone got a posthole digger?" The men scattered to get their supplies as Pa paced out the projected fence line, drawing the toe of his boot in the dirt.

"Johnny! We need your help over here!" Johnny turned to see Sergeant Bishop calling him. Beside him, another sergeant eyed Johnny like he was taking his measure. Pa waved Johnny off and he ran over to them.

Sergeant Bishop clapped a big hand on Johnny's

shoulder. "This here's Sergeant Jones, our artillery expert." Johnny bent his head back to look up at Sergeant Jones.

"Sergeant Bishop tells me you keep your head under fire." Sergeant Jones's gruff voice boomed through a great bushy beard. Johnny snatched off his hat and stood straighter. Sergeant Jones was all army, no mistaking that.

"My gun crews are well-trained, but I need a couple of men to handle our ammo and keep the gun positioned. You willing?"

"Yes, sir. Just tell me what to do and how to do it." Johnny's back stiffened and he pushed his shoulders back. "Got a rifle, too, if you need it." It sure would beat digging postholes. He felt stronger and braver already, working under competent men like Jones and Bishop.

"Good. We have six cannons, yonder four placed in fixed positions and two howitzers we can move as needed." Sergeant Jones pointed out the placement of the big guns, then turned to Sergeant Bishop. "He's your man now. You'll have to train him quicklike." With a curt nod to them both, Jones hurried off.

Sergeant Bishop tapped Johnny's stiff shoulder. "Come on along. I'll need to learn you the workings of a cannon right smart." Bishop grinned. "My boys'll help." He headed off toward his gun emplacement at a brisk pace, Johnny trotting to keep up. He'd learn fast. How hard could it be?

Twilight fast fading, lanterns lit small areas where groups of men worked at various tasks. Farmers were busy building the corral. The sutler, a civilian provisioner, led a crew bringing water from the creek, filling every bucket and barrel available. Eliza Mueller, across the parade ground by the stone barracks, directed a group of women cooking food for refugees. Ma and Amy carried stacks of towels from the adjacent laundry shed to the barracks.

Sergeant Bishop noticed Johnny's observation. "There's about three hundred settlers here now. Mrs. Mueller's got things well in hand over there, besides doing nursing duties for the doctor. Busy lady."

Walking past drilling soldiers, Johnny said, "I see reinforcements arrived. Looks to be more than Lieutenant Sheehan would have brought back."

"We now have about one hundred eighty 'effectives' armed and organized. Just over one hundred in companies B and C." Sergeant Bishop pointed to the far end of the quadrangle. "Over yonder are fifty Renville Rangers from St. Peter. Tom Galbraith had recruited them for the War Between the States." He pointed out another group of men drilling, not in uniform. "Over there's about twenty-five civilian volunteers and refugees. Armed."

"What about reinforcements from Fort Snelling? Any arrived yet?" It still didn't look to be enough soldiers, thought Johnny. There ought to be more.

The sergeant frowned. "Not yet. Lieutenant Sheehan thinks our first messenger didn't get through. He sent out Iron Face this morning. Best scout we've got."

"Sir! Loaded and ready!" said one of Bishop's men as Bishop and Johnny came up to the big gun. He stood beside the cannon, a long pole with some kind of device at its end held at attention like a rifle.

"Right. Johnny, stand there," Bishop indicated. "By tomorrow morning, you'll be an artilleryman." The gun crew laughed, evidently relishing teaching the new recruit.

"And by tomorrow night, you'll be an *experienced* artilleryman," said a grinning blue-coated young soldier. He made a space for Johnny behind the gun, where no barricade impeded its movement. "Don't stand too close. It jumps around quite a bit when the powder explodes."

THE BATTLE OF
FORT RIDGELY

August 22, 1862

From atop the rough cedar-shingled roof of Headquarters/Surgeons' Quarters, Johnny was doing sentry duty with Joe, a civilian scout. Joe Coursolle had arrived at the fort with his wife and baby son the previous morning. He wore a bright calico shirt, a red wool strip around his black hair, and a big bowie knife stuck under his belt. He must be a voyageur, Johnny figured. He turned his attention to the tall prairie grass. Mist slowly rose as the warm morning sun steamed the dew.

Joe had a spyglass and was scanning the countryside for movement. "Did you know the Dakota are capturing or killing all us mixed-bloods? Killing us because our ma or pa is white."

Mixed-bloods were being killed? *Chaska's a captured half-blood—is he in danger?*

Joe seemed lost in his own thoughts. "I'm worried about my two little daughters."

"Why? What happened?" Johnny was getting more anxious by the minute.

Joe still had eye to spyglass. "My dog Duta woke me before dawn the day of the Agency attack. Many braves, painted for war, were creeping past my house. I quietly hurried my family to the river, but my canoe was too small for all of us. I hid my girls in the rushes and told them I would be back after I had paddled their mama and baby brother across." Joe lowered the spyglass and put his hand over his brow as if to shade his eyes from the sun. "When I returned . . ." His whisper trembled, barely audible. "They were gone. Captured. Duta's barks would have alerted the braves to my girls' presence. So to protect their hiding place, I had to strangle my dog." Joe sounded like he was strangling, too.

Aghast, Johnny mumbled, "Maybe they're safe with the Indian women in Little Crow's camp. They're . . ." Sudden movement far out on the prairie caught Johnny's attention. "Joe, what's that?"

Joe shot up on his elbows, turned, and yelled to the soldiers below. "They're coming!" A bugle call instantly sounded the alert across the parade ground. Lieutenant Sheehan scrambled up the ladder beside them and reached for Joe's spyglass.

The Dakota, like a streaming herd of buffalo, converged in plain sight out on the prairie. There were

many bands, hundreds and hundreds of painted warriors. Johnny's already-tense muscles tightened from
his neck all the way down his spine. Little Crow had
succeeded in getting other tribes to join him.

Conferring together, the chiefs dispersed their
braves into the ravines surrounding three sides of the
fort. The lieutenant raised up and pointed. "I see Little
Crow. There, on the white horse. He's signaling he
wants to parlay."

"Don't trust him!" Sergeant Bishop yelled up.
"Remember the ferry ambush!"

Johnny spotted Little Crow, his white horse dotted
and decorated with war paint.

He inched farther up the roof, squinting. Was that a
pinto pony behind Little Crow? Could that be Chaska's
pony Lightfoot? Could Chaska be out there? Johnny
wished he had the spyglass. He shook his head. Chaska
would never join the war on whites. Some brave had
probably stolen his horse.

Joe crept up beside him and whistled softly. "There's
a lot of chiefs out there. Little Crow got many bands
together." Indians continually streamed toward them
across the prairie. Joe pointed east. "There's the
Wahpeton tribe." Then south. "Sisseton. They're coming at us from all sides."

Johnny watched steadily. Little Crow had organized

them. This had become war.

"We're ready for them," muttered Lieutenant Sheehan, climbing back down the ladder. Johnny and Joe scrambled down too, taking their posts alongside Sergeant Bishop at the southeast corner of the fort. Replacement sentries scrambled up.

Johnny hunkered down alongside the big cannon carriage, behind the large wooden-spoked wheel. There was precious little shelter. He watched and waited. He couldn't see much or hear much down on the ground. Getting impatient, Johnny stretched his neck up for a quick look and pulled back down. There was nothing coming yet. The wait grew longer. His calves cramped and he rubbed his legs.

Johnny worried why the Indians weren't attacking. What was taking so long? They greatly outnumbered the whites. Surely they weren't hesitating.

His mind scampered back to the pinto pony behind Little Crow. That couldn't have been Chaska. He shifted his weight from one bent leg to another.

Suddenly, a volley of shots at the far opposite corner of the fort shattered the watchful stillness. Johnny jerked his head around, rising up on his knees, too far away to see anything. He could hear, though. He heard Dakota warriors heading toward Sergeant McGrew's cannon emplacement, screaming terrifying war cries.

He heard a roar of exploding powder and saw smoke erupt from the great gun barrel. He heard Lieutenant Gere's riflemen add a steady barrage of gunfire. Within seconds, McGrew's twelve-pound howitzer roared again, a deafening blast, and Indian war whoops changed to terrified screams.

"Ready!" Sergeant Bishop shouted over the din. Startled, Johnny swiveled back to the ravine facing him. Furious painted warriors swarmed up, brandishing rifles and bows and arrows. They charged head-on toward Sergeant Bishop's big gun. Johnny felt like the entire charge was headed directly at him.

His gunnery mate placed his long lanyard to the touch hole, igniting the powder in the big Napoleon cannon. The ground quaked under him with the explosion, and the air shuddered around him. His ears splitting, Johnny leapt up and grabbed the heavy carriage wheel and shoved the cannon back into position, snatching a smoky breath. His crewmates jammed powder into the barrel and dropped in a canister shot.

Through clearing smoke, Johnny saw the attacking braves draw back. Were the braves retreating after one cannon shot? But immediately another charge rose up out of the south ravine, this time headed toward Sergeant Jones's emplacement at Johnny's right. They were everywhere at once! Attacking, falling back, attacking another position. Jones's cannon roared, followed by rifle fire from the Renville Rangers.

Joe Coursolle dodged in next to Johnny, firing his rifle into grassy humps and mounds. "The Dakota have good reason to worry about the fifty half-blood Rangers. They don't miss many shots." He fired at a treetop and dropped a sniper.

His attention back on the ravine, Johnny reached for his rifle, tucked under the big carriage. Johnny took quick aim and fired. If Joe could pick them off, so could he.

"There ain't fifty of them here anymore. Three ran off this morning and joined the war party. They tried to sabotage the cannon before they left. Stuffed it with rags," continued Joe.

The massed Indian assaults abruptly stopped. All the braves broke off and retreated to the ravines. Soon fierce shouting sprang up from the gullies. Johnny looked to Sergeant Bishop. Were the Indians fighting among themselves down in the ravine?

A vicious grin split the sergeant's face. "Hear that? The chiefs are furious at their warriors for retreating. Found out they can't charge a cannon. I bet they'll change their battle plan."

He was right. When the warriors swarmed out of the ravines again, they scattered individually, surrounding the fort on all sides. They seemed to melt into the earth, becoming grass and brush, becoming invisible. Then suddenly, a barrage of flaming arrows erupted from behind hillock and hump and grassy clumps, raining down on the roofs of the fort's buildings.

Bishop stood behind the bulk of his cannon, watching the arrows fly and fall.

"They'll go out. Everything's soaking wet from last night's rainstorm."

Most of the little fires did go out. But Johnny and Joe craned their necks when a fiery arrow landed on the roof of Headquarters directly above them. A curl of black smoke thickened, ringlets of flame twirled up. Lieutenant Sheehan yelled at Joe, "Grab an ax and go pound that out!"

Joe, jaws clenched, stuck his ax handle under his belt and scrambled up the ladder, his red shirt as blatant as a woodpecker on an ironwood tree. Ducking and dodging a flurry of bullets and arrows, whacking frantically at the stubborn flames, Joe quickly beat out the fire.

"Get down outta there!" Johnny yelled up, bracing the foot of the ladder.

Joe flopped to his stomach and rolled off the roof, landing with a soft thump in the wet earthworks right next to Johnny. He sat up, dazed. He patted his chest, arm, and legs. "Not even scratched," he marveled.

Johnny shakily handed him his rifle.

"Load the case shot," yelled Bishop. Crewmen reached back to the limber, which carried the ammunition, and passed it forward to the gunnery crew. "Ready, fire!" Bishop called. With a smoking belching roar, the cannon flung an exploding ball over the braves, scattering shrapnel into the grassy cover. Johnny stood back and covered his ears, coughing and choking on the dust and smoke. He pushed and jerked at the caisson's wheels, keeping it positioned. Joe aimed, shot, and reloaded his rifle, aimed, shot, and reloaded, providing covering fire to the gun crew.

"We need more powder!" Sergeant Bishop yelled. "Johnny, Joe, go for it."

Johnny stared at Joe. "Go for it? Go where?"

"Follow me." Joe laid his rifle down and raced across the parade ground, Johnny right on his heels, skirting Pa's corral full of bellowing sheep, bawling cows, and neighing horses. Reaching the northwest gun emplacement, Johnny gasped out to Sergeant McGrew what Bishop wanted.

McGrew nodded, quickly motioning three of his own men over. "We're low on ammo, too. You'll all have to make a run to the ammunition magazine. Bring back all the powder you can carry." Looking where McGrew pointed, Johnny's face turned dead white.

Two hundred yards of open grassland stood between the fort perimeter and the squat log building that housed the ammunition. "We'll cover you," shouted McGrew. "Now go!

Bent low, Johnny, Joe, and McGrew's three men raced off, dodging and zigzagging toward the ammunition hut. McGrew's cannon roared above them, shot exploding every twenty or so seconds into the ravine beyond them. Johnny ran full out through long tangled grass, hoping he wouldn't trip. He reached the heavy oak door first, pulled the latch, and shoved his shoulder against it. Hinges screeched as the door swung inward, and the men dashed inside the low-roofed walls. Johnny blinked several times, eyes adjusting to the dark interior. Stacked along the walls were barrels of black powder. "I sure hope this place doesn't take a flaming arrow," he gasped out.

"Take as much as you can carry," said Joe. "We don't want to do this again."

Whoomph! Canister shot exploded just outside. Johnny grabbed two small barrels, tucked them awkwardly under his arms and dashed back outside with the others toward McGrew, who had raised his sights and fired over them again. Arms and legs shaking, Johnny ducked behind the smoking cannon, coughing on the powder-laden air.

McGrew scarcely glanced at him. "There're Indians shooting from the outbuildings—getting close in! Aim at the sutler's cabin!" he yelled to his gun crew. Hands on his knees, gasping for a breath of clear air, Johnny raised his head to watch. A large group of braves had occupied the log houses just beyond the commissary, giving them a closer and more protected range to fire from than the ravine. McGrew aimed his cannon directly at the log cabins and fired. Again. And again. Each ball exploded into another small outbuilding with a fiery whoomph, scattering the braves.

Johnny and Joe hoisted two powder barrels apiece and ran back to their own post, gingerly setting them on the limber wagon and scooting back to their firing positions. Massed attacks from the ravines seemed to have stopped, and Johnny's breathing settled down. The firing stayed steady, but less intense. Looking out from behind his cannon, Johnny frowned. Shadows stretched long across the grass. He looked at the western sky. Could it be mid-afternoon already?

Just then, Eliza Mueller and the Humphrey boy scurried across the porch of the officers' quarters toward them and dodged into the shelter of the wagon box barricade beside their cannon crew. "Ammunition," she said, motioning young Hans to plunk down a case of canister shot on the limber wagon. "And coffee."

With a calm smile, she poured from a large steaming enamel pot she carried into a tin cup that passed from man to man.

Sergeant Bishop took a swallow. "How's the ammunition lasting? How much canister shot is left—how much case shot? We're going through it pretty fast."

Eliza took a drink of the coffee herself as she sat against the wagon box. "I've got some ladies making more in the barracks." She smiled over her tin cup. "We're cutting up iron rods I got from the blacksmith into quarter-inch slugs." Johnny felt heartened, watching her. She must be the calmest, steadiest person at the fort.

Bishop nodded. "How are the other positions holding up? Many casualties?"

Johnny's heart thumped. His family—were they all right?

"Very few," Eliza replied. "Two of Sheehan's men were shot during the first assault, till they fanned out for cover. Only one other killed since then, I believe." She paused a minute, thinking. "Whipple's cannon exploded a ball very close to Little Crow. He may have been wounded; no one's spotted him since then."

At the mention of Little Crow, Johnny's thoughts jerked back to Chaska. *Surely he isn't out there in the ravines, fighting against us.*

Suddenly Eliza stood and gathered her skirts in both hands. She leapt as light as a doe onto the porch of Headquarters, toward Sergeant Jones's cannon emplacement at the opposite end of the building.

What was she doing? Johnny looked back and saw massed warriors creeping into the log stables in back of Headquarters. "Sergeant! They're into the stables!" said Eliza. "The army mules and horses are still there." Before anyone could react, a barely contained stampede was herded out toward the ravines. Warriors fired from stable windows at the exposed gun crews. Within minutes, the warriors had taken all the animals and had secured a major building.

Sergeant Bishop's crew quickly realigned the caisson, aiming at the stables. While shoving the wheel hub into position, Johnny glimpsed Eliza running back toward them across the verandah. Halfway back, she stopped abruptly at the central hallway that divided Headquarters from the surgeon's quarters. She opened the door into the hallway and waited.

At the far end of the verandah, Jones's gun crew struggled to get their howitzer up the steps and onto the verandah. Johnny didn't get it. Why on earth were they moving the howitzer? And onto the porch? He looked back at Eliza holding the door open.

"Johnny!" yelled Sergeant Jones, beckoning him.

"Give us a hand here!" One wheel was up on a step, the other tottering.

"Sergeant!" Johnny yelled at Bishop, pointing to Sergeant Jones's struggling crew.

"Go help them!" Bishop hollered back.

Johnny jumped up, ran across, and grabbed hold of the caisson, helping manhandle the cannon onto the verandah and to the doorway Eliza held open. They positioned the cannon to point right down that hallway. Johnny stood panting over the gun barrel he had helped put in place. That's it, he thought. They're going to shoot through the passageway.

Eliza ran into and down the long dark hall to a door at the other end. She clutched its latch, turning and watching Jones for a signal.

Jones's voice boomed over the long steel barrel. "Pull it open, Eliza!" Johnny saw her jerk the latch at the far end and crouch back against the wall. Through the opened doors, directly in Jones's sights, were the stables. "Fire!" he hollered. The ball flew through the narrow hallway and out the opposite doorway. The force of the contained cannon shot shook the entire building.

With a thunderous whoomph and wallop, the cannonball hit the stable wall, smashing completely through it. The massive explosion ignited the hay and straw, instantly engulfing the log building in flames. Indians poured out every door and window, fleeing to the ravines. Johnny's heart hammered in his ears. He could hardly believe it had worked. Sergeant Jones and Eliza had stopped that attack in a heartbeat.

Eliza straightened her apron with a few pats, took young Humphrey's hand, and went back to her ammunition rounds. Bishop and Jones realigned their caisson, and the battle settled into a steady exchange of rifle fire. Long hot afternoon hours stretched out with the lengthening shadows. Relentless heat and clamoring gunshots layered the air.

Johnny sniffed something other than gun smoke. Was it wood smoke? Had a flaming arrow hit a rooftop without someone noticing? He looked back into the parade ground, at all the fort buildings. Nothing in the fort was on fire, but beyond the building to the west haystacks and woodpiles burned fiercely. Heavy thick clouds of smoke billowed around and through the fort. The Indians must have set them on fire. But why would they set haystacks afire?

Joe scrambled up to the roof to see above the smoke. "There's Chief Mankato. And Big Eagle. They're massing their braves in the southwest ravine." He turned and yelled down, "They're using the smoke for cover. They're going to attack from the southwest!"

Sergeant Jones's deep voice boomed clear across the parade ground, "Bishop! Help me haul that mobile cannon over to the fort entrance." He yelled over to an adjacent emplacement, "O'Shea! Bring your cannon to the entrance! We'll both fire west on my order! Double charge!"

"You heard Jones!" Bishop hollered to Joe and Johnny, pointing them to the center of the parade ground where another twelve-pounder sat awaiting action. "Give a hand with that big howitzer!"

Hell-bent-for-leather, Joe and Johnny took off, meeting Jones's crew at the gun site. Jones grabbed the foremost wheel, the others shoved their shoulder against the axle and the opposite wheel, hauling and heaving the heavy gun to Jones's new position. "Alert McGrew!" Jones ordered Johnny.

Johnny ran ahead, yelling, "Load your twenty-four pounder with double-shot! Jones's orders." He and Joe dropped into McGrew's gun pit, helping swivel the caisson wheels.

Three cannons now aligned southwest, McGrew's huge gun looming over the others. Three crews rammed powder and shot down the barrels, then rammed another shot down on top of it. They straightened and stood back, all attention on the sergeant.

"Lower the sights. We won't see them through this

smoke till they're practically on us." In seconds, McGrew's crew stood ready, waiting for the order to fire. Johnny's eyes burned from the smoke. He coughed and choked.

"FIRE!" yelled Sergeant Jones.

"FIRE!" hollered Sergeants McGrew and O'Shea.

Earsplitting blasts of the massed cannons shook every building and tree and rock and hill near the fort. Roars and rumbles reverberated through the valley and ravines. Dirt and dust flew through the smoke clouds like dry hailstones.

Immediately, the gun crews reloaded the cannons, waiting tensely for another order. But through breaks in the smoke, Johnny saw another shot would not be necessary. The hundreds of braves that had massed on the prairie and invaded the ravines now fled in wild disorder. Gun smoke and wood smoke that had engulfed the fort in heaping billows gradually drifted away over the wide prairies and wooded ravines.

Johnny stood with the artillery crews, the riflemen, the civilian defenders of Fort Ridgley, watching the Dakota retreat. Retreat without order or direction.

AFTERMATH
August 22, 1862

Johnny hung on the heavy caisson wheel, bracing himself against its solid iron, spasms quivering down his shaky legs. Pa came and put his arm around his shoulder and they leaned against each other. All around them, refugees streamed out of buildings, calling to each other, crying with joy and relief.

"I didn't know if we'd live through this day," said Pa. "Your Ma had a strong presentiment something really bad would happen."

"I wouldn't want to live through it again," Johnny rasped. Conversations punctuated with back-slapping and whoops and hollers surrounded them.

Pa glanced across the crowd. "I saw Chaska during the battle," he whispered to Johnny. "With Little Crow. Do you know anything about that?"

"I wasn't sure if I saw him or not. I only saw a pinto that looked like Lightfoot." Johnny gulped, sure that Pa wouldn't like what he had to tell him. "Chaska and I were both taken to Little Crow's village. I was released, but Chaska was expected to follow Little Crow."

Pa looked thunderstruck. He put his hand to his temple, rubbing it. "That needn't have happened," he said.

"I know, Pa. Chaska and I were both foolhardy." We aren't anymore, he thought.

"Other Day needs to know this." Pa massaged both temples.

"Chaska told me Other Day took Becky and a group of white settlers from the Upper Agency north. Perhaps to Hutchinson, perhaps as far as St. Paul."

Ma, skirts a-flying, ran into Pa's and Johnny's arms, then stepped back to brush dirt and gunpowder from their clothes. She flinched again at the sight of the long scab tracing Johnny's jawline. "You're not hurt? Neither one of you?"

"We're fine, Ma," said Johnny. He stood back and took a look at her. "You're a bit dusty, too. Where were you during the fighting?"

Ma gave him a sassy grin. "I'm the one who made your ammunition. It seems to have worked just fine."

"Was Amy with you cutting up iron rods?"

"No," said Ma. "She was with Eliza, tending the wounded." Ma looked around apprehensively. "She should have found us by now."

"Maybe someone was badly hurt," said Pa, "and still needs nursing."

Johnny looked through swirling smoke and dust, from the commissary to the barracks to Dr. Mueller's quarters. He stepped up onto an ammunition crate, looking over the crowd. He climbed up onto a wheel hub, to see farther. "Would she be at the barracks? Is that where the wounded were taken?"

Color drained from Ma's face. She barely nodded, both hands clutched over her heart. Johnny jumped down and raced to the barracks, shoving through knots of people, their celebration chilling his heart more than the war whoops had. Bursting through the door, he stopped short.

Eliza was bent over an unconscious soldier, cutting his uniform sleeve away from an arrow jutting out of his arm. Dr. Mueller was scrubbing his hands at a steaming basin. "If you're not bleeding to death, you'll be the next one treated," Eliza said over her shoulder, not looking to see who had entered.

"Eliza, where's Amy?" Johnny stared at the arrow and the slow dripping of blood.

Turning quickly, Eliza said, "With your mother, I assume." She brushed back a strand of hair, her hand smudging blood on her forehead. "Earlier this morning, they were tending a sick baby in the commissary."

She glanced at the doctor. "Did you see . . ."

Pa burst in the door. "She's not at the commissary."

Clutching Pa, Ma exchanged a panicked glance with Eliza, then her eyes rolled back in her head, and she slumped down. Johnny caught her, lowered her to a cot, and sat on its edge, his own knees trembling.

Dr. Mueller took Eliza's place alongside the soldier. "Tend to her," he said.

Eliza knelt alongside Ma. She wrung out a wet cloth and laid it across Ma's forehead. "Who last saw Amy?" Eliza glanced up at Pa and Johnny. "Where would she have been later this morning?"

Pa hovered over Ma, a furrow as deep as a plowshare creasing his brow. "She would have milked Bessie in the stable."

"But by mid-morning all the farm animals had been brought inside the parade ground," said Johnny. "Pa? I don't recollect Amy bringing Bessie."

Young Hans Humphrey stood wide-eyed in the doorway. "Bessie was balky," he blurted out. "She wouldn't leave the manger while there was still hay to eat and Amy was pulling her lead rope and I was pushing Bessie from behind and she was kicking at me when I'd try to push her and Amy told me to help herd the sheep up to the corral and that she would come as soon as Bessie finished eating and so I came back and then all the shooting started and I ran to Eliza. . . . "

Johnny rushed past him out to the corral and scrambled up to the top rail. The animals milled restlessly, shoving and crowding each other. Bessie wasn't among them.

Johnny gripped the fence rail. How long had Amy stayed at the stable? It was mid-afternoon when the Indians had taken it. He jumped to the ground.

Pa joined him at the fence rail. "Lieutenant Sheehan has ordered men to search the grounds for Amy." His voice cracked. "If she stayed too long at the stable, the Indians could have taken her."

"No!" Images of Little Crow's village, the fires, the cries of the wounded captives, assaulted Johnny's senses. "She's hiding somewhere. In a tree. Under a ravine bank. Too scared to come out." He glanced frantically around the grounds, past the barricades. "We need to find tracks—any traces at all—outside the fort. Around the stable."

Pa nodded curtly, and he and Johnny strode to Headquarters, out through the open central hallway to the smoldering stable ruins behind.

Staring into still-burning logs, another thought slammed into Johnny's mind.

"Could Amy have hidden somewhere in the stable when the Indians came? Would she still have been hiding in there when the cannon fire hit it?"

"Not likely." Pa shook his head as if to eliminate that possibility. "If we don't find any other trace of her, we'll sift through the ashes." He kept shaking his head.

Johnny bit his lip till he tasted salty blood and turned away from the huge crackling log pile. Pushing through scorched grass, stomping down cinder piles, he finally located tracks. "Here, Pa! Heading to the ravine!" Following the trail down the steep wooded slopes, scrambling and sliding, he and Pa traced hoof prints that mingled with moccasin prints that all mashed together in the mud where a creek flowed. Trampled brush and broken tree limbs and branches covered all sign of individual tracks. There was no way to sort them out or to follow them.

Johnny thought he might throw up, his stomach churned so.

Pa didn't sound so good, either. "They've all left. Taken their wounded and dead with them. Maybe took Amy, too."

Still they searched, soldiers and refugees joining them through the ravines on all sides of the fort. Up trees and under banks and in thickets and around rock piles and through tangled briar patches. They found not a trace of Amy. Shadows lengthened, shrouding the steep ravines in deepening darkness.

Finally, in the black of night, in the empty darkness of his heart, Johnny realized it was no use. If Amy were near, he would know it. If she had been in the fire, he would feel it. He dragged his feet up the muddy slopes, following Pa. "Maybe Other Day can find out what happened. Where she is . . ."

Pa didn't stop or look back at Johnny. "Little Crow will know Other Day rescued whites at the Upper Agency. That makes Other Day his enemy."

"But Chaska is still in Little Crow's village." Johnny forced confidence into his voice. "He'll protect her. Star Woman will take care of her. She has authority in the village. . . . "

His voice suddenly fell silent, cut off in mid-thought. Star Woman's authority depended on Other Day's influence. If Other Day were branded a traitor, Chaska and Star Woman and Raven would all be helpless. And so would Amy.

DAKOTA DISCORD
August 28, 1862

About a week later, Johnny sat on a plank bench, his back against the commissary wall. It was hot, the dog days of summer, and he was glad it was Joe and not himself doing lookout duty on the roof. He was glad, too, that there'd been no more attacks on the fort.

He ramrodded an oil rag down his gun barrel, wiping out powder residue. There still was plenty to worry about, though. His heart ached for Amy, and there was no way he could stop his thoughts of what might be happening to her. He held the rifle up and sighted down the barrel, his finger at the other end. The reflected light on his finger shone bright and round.

Ma was frantic—not eating much, fidgety, and anxious. She didn't like having Pa or Johnny out of her sight for long. The worst part, Johnny thought, was that there was nothing they could do to find Amy. He rubbed the gun stock with an oiled rag, wishing there was something he could do. But search parties would be useless—they couldn't search the entire countryside. And troops could not be spared.

He hadn't heard any more of Chaska, either. Lord only knew where he was, what he was doing, or what might have happened to him.

"Johnny, haul yourself up here!" Joe's red-banded head poked over the edge of the commissary roof, his arm pointing down the fort road. "Yonder's a half-breed Indian, wanting you. You know him?"

Scrambling up the ladder, Johnny sprawled down next to Joe and grabbed his spyglass, fixing his sight on the figure mounted on the black and white pinto pony. Relief flooded through him like rapids over river rocks. There sat Chaska, waiting within calling distance but beyond shooting distance. "Sure do know him—I'd been hoping he'd come by." Tossing the spyglass back to Joe, he scooted down the ladder, jumped on the nearest saddled horse, and galloped out the fort entrance.

Johnny pulled up alongside Chaska and gripped his wrist. "Do you know where Amy is? Who has her?"

The edges of Chaska's mouth turned up in a slight smile. "She is safe. Amy was brought in as a captive. Star Woman traded her pony for her, and made it known in the village that Amy is now her child."

Alive and well and protected. Johnny released

Chaska's arm. "And what about you? How did you get away from Little Crow?"

Chaska's smile disappeared. "I was forced along on the Fort Ridgely attack, but I would not fight. Little Crow was furious but dared not harm the son of Other Day. Although that night at the Warrior's Lodge, he poured shame on me. He scorned my lack of skill and daring. He said he'd spared the life of a coward. Yesterday he sent me with Cut Nose and his raiding party, saying that if I did not return with a white scalp, Cut Nose would return with mine."

Johnny's blood chilled, shivers ran through his veins. He'd never seen Chaska so angry.

"As easily as stalking a deer, I slipped past them as they slept. They thought the son of Other Day too cowardly to try an escape." Scorn dripped from Chaska's voice like blood from his skinning knife. "I could have had *their* scalps." He lifted high a quiver of arrows with a grin that did nothing to warm Johnny's blood. "Stealing a weapon yet leaving a life untouched is a coup worthy of an eagle feather."

Willing his lips to be firm and his gaze steady, Johnny smiled back. "No one can ever doubt your bravery or your skill. Who could scorn you now?" His lip trembled ever so slightly. *And who would protect Amy now?*

Chaska's manner softened as he sifted Johnny's

thoughts. "There are still many friends of Other Day in Little Crow's camp. Star Woman is strong. Raven is quick. Amy is brave and smart."

Johnny ducked his head, hiding embarrassment. Chaska always knew what he was thinking, always had an answer before Johnny asked a question. The warmth in Chaska's voice flowed back through Johnny's body and his spirit and his resolve. None of the terrible things that had happened had changed their friendship. He looked at Chaska, his smile genuine. "What happens next?"

Like a sudden squall chasing fair weather, Chaska's face darkened. "Take me to the commanding officer. I bring information about Little Crow."

Trotting back to the fort, Johnny spotted his waiting parents and the Muellers. The grin on his face foretelling good news, he shouted, "Amy is safe and protected with Star Woman." Ma buried her face in Pa's shoulder, sobs shaking her. Pa held her, nodding at both Chaska and Johnny, relief all over his face. "Join us at Headquarters," Johnny called.

Lieutenant Sheehan looked up from his desk, quickly laid down his quill pen and blotted his paper. He stood and stretched out his hand to Chaska. "Good to see you, Chaska. The Preusses have told me of your father's rescue efforts at the Upper Agency." Johnny glanced at Pa, remembering their conversation with Captain Marsh in this same room. That had not gone well at all.

Sheehan sat down behind the desk, indicating that his visitors should take the facing chairs.

Chaska sat between Johnny and his pa, his back straight as the ladder-back chair. "I bring news of Little Crow and the white captives." The lieutenant leaned forward eagerly, hands clasped before him. "I come directly from the Upper Agency. Many of us farmer Indians have stayed in the homes of our white friends to prevent burning or looting. But yesterday, Little Crow arrived. He brought his entire village up the river."

Johnny and Pa exchanged a quick glance. Without actually saying so, Chaska implied he had been staying at the Upper Agency when Little Crow arrived. But Johnny was sure Chaska had still been Little Crow's prisoner. That Little Crow had brought Chaska along with him.

Lieutenant Sheehan's eyebrows raised at Chaska's news. "Little Crow's camp has moved to the Upper Agency? He moved the entire village? That's several hundred people, including the women and children." He steepled his fingers. "That explains why we haven't seen any Indian activity around here the last few days. Why did Little Crow decide to relocate?"

"Because he heard that Long Trader, whom you call Colonel Sibley, is coming after him with great numbers of white soldiers."

Lieutenant Sheehan snorted. "We've been hearing that, too, but haven't seen a trace of Sibley yet. It's been eight days since we first sent to Fort Snelling for help."

Chaska shrugged slightly. "Reaching the Upper Agency, Little Crow went first to the Yellow Medicine reservation, demanding that the Dakota bands there join his war against the whites. But Little Paul, chief of the Mdewakanton band, refused. He said his people would not fight the whites. That they would fight against Little Crow's band before they would war on whites."

This news startled Johnny. He'd known about the peace party early on, but assumed the Dakota had all joined together once the attacks started.

"They refused to join Little Crow?" Lieutenant Sheehan stared at the distant wall, pondering this news. "At the risk of starting a war among the tribes?"

"Little Paul did much more than refuse Little Crow. He made demands of his own. First, that Little Crow turn his captives over to Little Paul so that he could return them unharmed to the whites. He demanded that Little Crow leave his territory and take his band north to Canada or west to Dakota Territory."

Johnny's thoughts nearly exploded out of his mouth, but he managed to clamp his jaw shut. Then what had happened to Amy? Did Little Crow turn her over to Little Paul? Or was Amy taken along to Canada or Dakota Territory?

"Little Crow's anger swept the camp like prairie fire," said Chaska, his own eyes ablaze. "Fighting nearly broke out between their bands. But Little Crow realized he could not war against both the Mdewakanton and Long Trader's soldiers. He left Little Paul's village and settled his camp across the river."

Pa broke in, facing Chaska directly. "Did Little Crow keep his captives? Is Amy with them?"

Chaska turned to Pa, his expression relaxing. "Little Paul managed to secure only a few of the captives, mixed-bloods he claimed were relatives of his band. But the rest, including Amy, remain with Little Crow. He says they will suffer along with his own people if Long Trader pursues him and he is forced to flee westward."

Johnny gripped the edge of his chair. Now all Amy had was Star Woman's protection. What influence did she still hold? He held desperately to Chaska's reassurance earlier that Amy was safe. He must trust Chaska's confidence.

Lieutenant Sheehan leaned back, tilting his chair. "Interesting. The Sioux are divided among themselves.

There are whole bands that refuse to join Little Crow, that will fight against him and his war."

"The Dakota are in fact divided three ways," continued Chaska. "Besides the war party and the peace party, there is a neutral party. There are many tribes who want no part of this war. They refuse to fight with Little Crow and they refuse to fight against him."

Johnny tried to figure out Chaska's stand through all this. Just by being here, telling all this, Chaska evidently had decided to side with the whites. Had he given up his Indian sympathies completely? He had felt so strongly.

"What does Little Crow plan to do next?" asked Lieutenant Sheehan.

"He will divide his remaining forces," said Chaska. "Little Crow will lead one group north, probably to Fort Abercrombie, and the other chiefs will most likely raid settlements to the southeast."

The lieutenant's hands flattened on his desk. He shook his head. "They'll be all over the countryside. We need troop strength if we are to stop them. Where in Hades are Colonel Sibley's forces? They should have left Fort Snelling days ago. My runner made it to Fort Snelling in eighteen hours!"

As if in answer to his question, an outside sentry yelled, "Mounted troops coming on the St. Peter road!"

The lieutenant bolted from his chair and out the door, stopping abruptly on Headquarters' porch steps to straighten his uniform. Pa, Johnny, and Chaska stood behind him, the verandah offering a good viewpoint to await the troops' arrival.

Soldiers and refugees streamed out of all the buildings, gathering at Fort Ridgely's entrance, waving their arms and cheering as the advance guard approached.

Johnny, his shoulder touching Chaska's, watched the column of horse soldiers ride into the parade ground and line up in front of Headquarters. Row upon row of troops formed in ranks behind them, hundreds of soldiers, mounted and foot, troop wagons and supply wagons.

An Indian scout astride a speckled-rump horse sat beside the commanding officer at the head of the troops. Johnny threw a glance at Chaska. The scout noticed them and dipped his lance at them. "It's Other Day." Chaska acknowledged his father's greeting with a nod and a smile he could not seem to suppress.

"It appears Other Day is now Colonel Sibley's personal scout." Pa flashed an even bigger smile at his old friend and neighbor.

Sunlight glinted blindingly off the soldiers' fixed bayonets as troops continued to stream in the fort entrance, crowding the parade ground, standing smartly at attention beneath the battered and ragged United States flag. Johnny put his hand over his chest, not just to honor the flag but to calm the wild exuberant beating of his heart.

BURIAL DETAIL
August 31–September 1, 1862

After reveille, Johnny and Chaska found a place in the mess hall and settled themselves on the rough plank seats. The stocky young private seated there reached across the table and shook their hands. "I'm Dennis Felix. Company A, Sixth Minnesota." He brushed a few cornbread crumbs off his spanking new uniform.

Johnny shoved his fork into the beans on his tin plate. "So where have your troops been the last week or so? We sure could have used your help."

"We spent the last several days at St. Peter, doing nothing but drilling and waiting on field supplies." Dennis stirred sugar into his coffee, clanking his spoon against the cup. "Colonel Sibley sends a letter to St. Paul every day, complaining to no end about not having enough wagons and rifles and ammunition. Hunkers down and refuses to go anywhere until he's mustered a force large enough to take into battle, which I hope will be right soon. We're wanting to give those

Sioux some real grief." He slurped a long sweet swallow, then met Chaska's eyes across the table. He shrugged slightly, evidently assuming that as Chaska was eating in an army mess hall, he felt the same way.

"Just how long has the Sixth Minnesota been soldiering?" asked Chaska, a bit of challenge in his voice. "Had any fighting experience?"

"Well, more than Colonel McPhail's volunteers have had. Most of them never held a rifle till a week ago." He grinned good-naturedly at Chaska.

"That kind of explains why Sibley's so intent on getting you boys fit, don't it?" Chaska grinned back.

Joe Coursolle, red bandanna askew over one eye, burst into the door and waved his arm at Chaska and Johnny. "Sibley's sending out a burial detail. Civilians are coming, too—to find family members. Get your gear." He dashed back outside, the door slamming behind him.

Johnny blinked rapidly. Burial detail?

Chaska leaned in close, speaking softly. "Everyone killed in the last two weeks is still lying out there—family and friends of the settlers here in the fort. There's lots of demands on Sibley to find them and bury them." He stood, leading Johnny out of the mess hall. "Let's go. Maybe we can find Amy's trail, and Grandmother's and Raven's."

≈≈

A short time later, Johnny again rode out of the fort with a column of soldiers, not at all sure he wanted to ride back along the Agency Road. Besides, Ma had been real upset with him leaving again, till Pa pointed out that more than one hundred seventy men made up this expedition, and seventeen horse-drawn wagons. And that they'd be gone only two days. It seemed safe enough, Pa had reckoned.

"Do you think we'll learn anything about the captives?" Johnny asked Chaska, not sure if he would answer. Major Brown had told Chaska to leave his Indian pinto behind and ride an army mule like the other scouts. Chaska had done so without comment, but had been tight-lipped since they'd left the fort. Johnny inclined his head toward the major leading the column. "The major's wife and family were captured, too. He's looking to gather information."

"I'm hankering to find a war party," said Joe, riding beside Chaska. "Get my girls back." Joe looked like a one-man war party himself, a feather tucked into his headband, his mule defiantly painted with red and yellow streaks.

Chaska shook his head impatiently. "It's not likely we'll find any captives. Brown's scouts claim there's no Dakota stalking anywhere near here. We're just out to find and bury the dead bodies."

Johnny shifted uneasily in his saddle, riding down the road they had taken with Captain Marsh. Like corn parching over a campfire, vivid images popped up in his head, of White Dog calling them across the river, of shots ripping into them from all directions, of hiding in the thicket, of Captain Marsh's drowning. He struggled to clamp a mental lid on the haunting sights.

"Company, halt!" Major Brown pulled up before a burned-out cabin, nettles and ragweed already sprouting up through ashes. A bad smell permeated the air. There was lots of buzzing in the air, too—black flies. Brown swore, turned in his saddle, and motioned to the men in the wagons behind him. The men climbed down, dragging shovels and pickaxes. Grasshoppers jumped ahead of them as they strode through the weeds.

Johnny tried to picture the shovels burying the gory images that kept resurfacing in his mind. He concentrated on the sounds, the clanking pickaxes and the thudding dirt. When finally the job was finished and they moved on, it was to another settler's cabin and more bodies. And then another. And yet another.

Johnny's arm and leg muscles knotted as the column rounded the bend that led to the river and the Redwood ferry. Strewn along the half mile of dirt road ahead sprawled dozens of long-dead bodies. Johnny could see that the soldiers had been stripped of their uniforms. He jerked on his horse's reins, his calves and forearms twitching. Johnny looked away, but he couldn't do much about the stink, or the industrious buzz of the black flies.

The soldiers buried over fifty bodies. As the burial party left along the Agency Road, they passed the long rows of mounded dirt. One of the men had made crosses out of sticks tied together with rawhide and stuck them in the ground.

Some time and distance later, Brown ordered camp set up for the night, near where Birch Coulee Creek burbled toward the river. Neither Johnny nor Chaska nor anyone else said much that evening, tending to chores without comment or complaint. Campfire smoke drifted across pointed tent rows, carrying aromas of coffee and biscuits and fried side pork. As twilight faded to starlit night, the breeze in the willows, the croaking of frogs, and the chirping of crickets gradually calmed Johnny's tense nerves. Stretched out on his blanket, head resting on his saddle, he slept.

~~~

"We're splitting into two parties," Chaska told Johnny the next morning. He tossed an army saddle onto his mule and reached under its belly for the cinch strap. "More bodies are being found than expected—two days won't get the job done. Captain Grant took his military escort along the north side of the river; we'll go with Major Brown into the Agency and on to where Little Crow had his village."

Johnny fitted his saddlebags and blanket across his horse's back and jerked the cinch tight. "Let's do what we have to do."

〰

Crossing at the Palmer ferry, the company approached the Lower Sioux Agency from the south. Johnny looked around, trying to get his bearings in the wide deserted meadow. All the stores and the cabins had been burned, nothing left but charred logs and stone foundations. No mistaking the smell, though.

"The stone warehouse is still standing," Chaska pointed out.

The group spread out, wandering off in groups of two or three, carrying shovels. Bodies were scattered over a wide area, many near the trader's store. Soon clanks of pickax and shovel and thuds of dirt clods broke the silence.

"You knew all these people; you should help identify them," said Chaska. "Folks will want to know who was killed and where they were buried." Johnny nodded, and they headed toward a group of soldiers crowded around a body sprawled in the tall grass. Chaska and Johnny rode up alongside. Flies flew up in swirling black whirlwinds. The body was riddled with bullet holes and feathered arrows. A hay scythe skewered up from his bloody chest. Grass stuffed his mouth.

Johnny's stomach lurched. He muttered to Chaska. "Trader Myrick. All these murders . . . all Myrick's fault. His and Galbraith's. They should have known that violence would result."

"That was just the flint that sparked the fire." Chaska spit out words like he'd bitten into bitter weeds. "All the government's lies, the cheating and stealing by agents and traders, year after year—all heaped up like deadwood stacked for burning."

After Johnny had identified most of the bodies, Chaska and Johnny led their mounts out of the settlement to Little Crow's village. A trampled clearing ringed by willow trees defined the deserted Indian camp. Chaska walked slowly down the beaten path. He inspected discarded belongings, kneeling once beside a fire pit to sift cold ashes through his fingers. He turned on his heels, studying the willow thicket. "They've been gone several days."

"Was this where Star Woman's teepee stood?" Johnny bent down too, and ran his hands through grassy clumps surrounding a trampled circle in the dirt.

He held up a small basket woven with a pattern of green pine needles. "Is this hers?"

Chaska took the basket from Johnny. Reaching inside, he lifted out a pair of unfinished deerskin moccasins, partially decorated with porcupine quills. "Little Crow left in a big hurry. Star Woman would not have discarded this." He rose and carefully fitted his grandmother's basket into a leather pouch thrown over his mule's withers. He stood quietly a moment, his head down.

Johnny bit his lip watching. How hard this must be for Chaska. He put his hand on Chaska's bent shoulder, hoping his touch would offer some slim comfort.

～～～

Toward evening, Major Brown's group met up with Captain Grant, whose soldiers were scurrying to set up camp near Birch Coulee Creek. Brown soon busied his men too, driving in tent stakes, tethering horses, starting campfires. The entire compound scuttled like beetles on a dung pile.

Chaska frowned as he surveyed the campsite, in no hurry to dismount and erect their tent. Johnny followed his gaze. What didn't Chaska like?

The lay of the ground was rolling, slight hills and valleys. There was a ravine on one side, in which Johnny could hear the creek splashing over rocks. A grove of birch trees on another side, a high mound of prairie grasses on the third.

"Bad site," said Chaska.

Johnny looked again. Cover, he noted. The ravines, the trees, the mounds, the tall weeds all provided cover. His horse stretched his neck down, reaching for the prairie grass. Joe trotted up to them, a frown furrowing his forehead right up into his headband. "I found fresh tracks downstream." He pointed toward the coulee. "And kinnickinnick bark shavings."

Johnny stared at Joe, alarm tingling his spine. Could Indians be near here? "Go tell Major Brown, or Captain Grant."

"Already did." Joe's voice snarled like a trapped muskrat. "Brown says there's no Indians within a hundred miles. Said we're as safe as if we were in our own featherbeds." He spat tobacco juice on the ground.

They sat awhile astride their mounts on a slight slope, surveying the surroundings and the camp. The company's seventeen wagons had been drawn into a large circle, tents in the middle, horses tethered to ropes between wagons, sentries posted. It all looked very military. Johnny's horse shook his head, restless, wanting to be fed.

"Dig a hole to sleep in," Joe growled. "Sleep with your rifle next to you. Loaded."

BIRCH COULEE
September 2, 1862

CRACK! CrackCrackCrackCrackCrack! Gunshots and screeching, screaming war whoops shattered the predawn stillness. The whistling swish of feathered arrows and crackling rifle fire set nesting birds squawking and cawing.

Johnny's head whipped up off his saddle and he rolled onto his stomach. He grabbed his gun and peered into the darkness. Panicked sentries raced toward them from their outposts and dove under the wagons, almost toppling into their sleeping pits. Bright flashes of gunpowder briefly illuminated dark shadows scurrying from every direction. Gunfire flashed closer and closer. From the tents behind him, chaotic shouts and screams broke out. Horses neighed and reared. People crashed into equipment and each other till a deep commanding voice hollered out, "Lay down on your bellies and shoot!"

"They're charging!" yelled Chaska. "Aim for the flashes."

Johnny's hands were clenched so tightly on his rifle he had to force his finger into the trigger guard. He had to make a conscious effort to sight and aim and then squeeze the trigger. Screams sounded behind him and before him, war whoops beyond him. Spotting a powder flash out in the blackness, he fired at it, but didn't know if he'd hit anything.

Johnny turned over onto his back to reload his rifle, facing the tether line. His jaw dropped open. Rearing, jerking against their ropes, neighing in panic, horses and mules crashed to the ground kicking and shrieking as arrows and bullets struck them.

"They're killing the horses!" Johnny yelled.

Chaska had noticed, too. "We can't escape or send for help." One after another, the horses fell, their screams dying with them.

"Form a breastworks!" shouted Captain Anderson. "Drag those dead horses around to make a barricade!"

Joe pulled Johnny's sleeve. "We got nothing to duck behind. Help me haul a horse back here." He crouched low and ran to the picket line and grabbed a leg of the closest dead horse. "Come on!" he called back.

Johnny chased after Joe, dodging kicks and flailing hooves from the few remaining living animals, and hauled on the horse's other leg. Chaska fired steadily, providing what cover he could. Pulling, pushing, shoving, dragging, Joe and Johnny wrestled the animal into position in front of their sleeping hollow. Johnny jumped down into his pit, hunkering down behind the horse carcass. He grabbed his rifle, steadied its barrel on the horse's back, aimed, and fired. He didn't need to concentrate on how to do it anymore.

Johnny stretched out to reach into his ammo bag for bullets but quickly pulled his legs up and out of the way. One last horse raced panic-stricken through the wagon enclosure, nearly trampling him. Suddenly Chaska darted past into the open, facing the crazed horse galloping down on him. He dodged its stampeding hooves and grabbed the horse's rope. Digging his heels into the dirt, he jerked the horse around, reaching for its halter. With an ear-piercing shriek, the horse crashed to the ground with a flailing thud. A sharpshooting warrior had just shot down all chance of sending for help. Chaska dashed back to his rifle pit.

The fierce battle gradually steadied into an exchange of gunshots as warriors stopped charging and dropped down behind the trees and the low hills to fire. That settled Johnny some—he'd done this before. It was easier to think without so many screams and war whoops ramming against his ears. The day was getting lighter; it was past dawn now.

As he turned again to reload, Johnny glanced

through the camp, now littered with dead men and horses. Huge red blotches and puddles of blood stood out starkly against dirt and dark uniforms and horse-hide. Johnny's eyesight blurred, seeing only splashes of red and black. A figure dashed through it, gaining shape and form as Johnny struggled to focus. It was Dr. Daniels.

The doctor raced from body to body, crouching, pressing his hand against each neck, bending his ear to every chest. Bent over a bleeding soldier, he raised his head and hollered, "I need help, here!" A civilian scooted to him through concentrated rifle fire, and together they hurriedly dragged the groaning man to their dead-horse-barricaded dugout. Captain Anderson, clutching his bloody arm, scurried from his pit to theirs.

Johnny turned back to the fighting. With the rising sun now in his eyes, he could barely see the tall prairie grasses and the birch trees bordering the coulee. He rubbed his eyes, wincing as sand and dust scratched against them. Blinking away cleansing tears, he looked across the waving grass. It was hard to make out rifle flashes in sunlight. He couldn't see anything to aim at.

"If they're using bow and arrow, they rise up to shoot," said Joe, lying next to him. "Snipers hide in the trees, too. Watch for feathers and war paint." He aimed his rifle up at leafy birch boughs and fired. A warrior crashed down, hitting the ground with a loud thunk.

Furious howls roared up off the surrounding slopes. "We saw you shoot, Hinhankaga! You killed the son of Traveling Hail! Now we will kill your daughters!"

Mouth agape, Johnny turned to Joe.

Joe stared into Johnny's gasping face. "Then they *are* alive!" Immediately, Joe's face contorted with dread. "And now they will kill them."

Retaliatory shots poured into their position from every direction, bullets shattering into wagon boxes. Splinters flew like arrowheads. Dennis, next to Joe, let out a yelp, grabbing at his cheek. Beyond him, a soldier pitched backward, shot in the head. Johnny jerked his attention back to the firing line, to staying alive.

Hours raced by, the hot sun burning a path across a clear sky. Dripping sweat stung Johnny's eyes as he squinted for another target, the neckerchief-sweatband tied around his forehead now saturated. Oddly, his mouth was dry as dust. He licked his parched lips. "We need water," he muttered.

"The horses kicked the buckets over." Chaska's lips barely moved.

"We're getting low on bullets too," said Joe. "Know where they're at, Dennis?"

Dennis sat back to reload, his hand scraping the bottom of his ammunition bag and coming out empty. He pointed clear across the encampment at an exposed wagon riddled with arrows and bullet holes. "The supply wagon's over yonder."

Chaska rolled up and out of the rifle pit, rasping, "Follow me. Stay down." Gun gripped in his hand, Chaska scurried off, fast and low like a stalking coyote.

They all stared after him. Johnny couldn't get his knees under himself. The supply wagon was a completely exposed target, the area surrounding it a shooting range.

Joe grimaced at Johnny. "It can't be no worse than running after powder at Fort Ridgely." He dashed off after Chaska. Dennis shuddered, then followed Joe.

A bullet splatted into the horse Johnny crouched next to, and Johnny flipped onto his stomach and scurried after Dennis, spitting out the dry dust the others stirred up.

Soon they all lay on their backs staring up at the underside of the supply wagon. "Now what?" asked Johnny, breathing hard.

"Raise your feet. Tip it over." Chaska wedged his boots against the edge of the wagon box. Johnny, Joe, and Dennis jammed their boots beside Chaska's and they all kicked up and out. The wagon rocked ahead and then back. "Again!" yelled Chaska. "Now!" Shoved up and forward, the wagon creaked, threatening to bust up, teetering. Johnny shoved his hands under his hips, pushing his legs higher, elbows bracing against the hard ground. Suddenly the weight lifted off his feet as the wagon crashed over onto its side, sideboards splintering and loaded boxes spilling out onto the ground.

Dennis yelled, "Get this stuff out of here before a bullet hits the powder." He crawled to the broken endgate and pulled ammunition boxes from the wagon. He shoved them toward Joe to Chaska to Johnny, now stretched apart. The crates passed rapidly from man to man along the firing line, each one taking a handful of bullets and sending the boxes on.

Johnny dragged the last box behind him back to his rifle pit. He pried the wooden cover off and scooped out a handful. He stopped and rubbed his gritty eyes with his free hand and looked closer at the hard round bullets. They didn't look right. He rolled them around in his palm. They didn't feel right, either. Johnny tipped the ammo box and checked the bore number. "These are .62 caliber. Our rifles are .58." Men all along the firing line shouted the same complaint.

Captain Grant ran over and dropped beside them. He poured a handful of bullets from one hand to the other and then flung them back into the ammo box. "Ordnance officer at the fort sent along the wrong ammo," he growled, his voice gritty as gravel. "Only thing you can do now is whittle them down with your knives."

He fixed a fierce gaze on Chaska and Johnny. "You two follow me."

Johnny and Chaska darted and dodged across the compound behind Captain Grant into Captain Anderson's tent. Major Brown sat in a camp chair; shirt half off as Dr. Daniels wound a bandage around his shoulder. Captain Anderson, arm in a sling, conferred with a couple of lieutenants and sergeants.

It was stifling hot inside, even though the canvas was riddled with bullet holes. No breeze stirred. A few blanket rolls piled around the edge provided meager protection from stray bullets and arrows.

Turning to include everyone, Captain Anderson took off his hat and wiped dirty sweat off his face with his arm. "Here's the status. Twenty-two men dead, all ninety horses shot. And we're pinned down; there's no way out."

Johnny's heart dropped to his stomach like a dirt clod down a gopher hole. They'd all be killed.

"Our campsite's too low—the Indians can see everything inside. They're picking us off from the trees and the hillocks," the captain continued. "We need higher barricades. Tip over all the wagons; fill the gaps with whatever we can pull out of them."

"Leave the one beside my tent," interrupted Dr. Daniels. "Mrs. Krieger's in it."

"What?" croaked Johnny. "Who?" No women had come along.

Dr. Daniels glanced over at Johnny. "We just found her yesterday, hiding in roadside brush. She'd been shot in the back and has a knife wound in her stomach. Somehow she survived an Indian attack two weeks ago." He shook his head as if even he couldn't believe it.

"But you can't leave her in the only standing wagon—an exposed target," argued Johnny.

"Moving her will kill her for sure," said the captain, his tone sharp as an arrow tip. "She's tucked around with rolled blankets and gear boxes." He looked from man to man. "Get the breastworks as high as you can. Pile up saddles, all the supplies." He again ran an arm across his face and wiped off dripping dirty sweat. "Pile the dead bodies up too," he said, his voice dropping an octave. "They can still give us protection."

Without a word, the lieutenants and sergeants left. Johnny stared after them, speechless. Pile up the dead bodies? Had he heard that right?

Behind him he heard Dr. Daniels ask, "What about food and water?"

Captain Grant replied, "It'll be sent around late afternoon."

Chaska spoke to Captain Anderson. "Sir, the battle sounds must have been heard back at the fort. Won't Colonel Sibley send reinforcements by then?"

"It's our only hope." Captain Anderson watched across the campsite as wagons crashed over, clamoring, clattering, and raising dusty billows. Dakota warriors' firing immediately intensified from the coulee and prairie hills.

Johnny and Chaska crept back to their positions through a choking layer of dust and gun smoke. Johnny didn't have enough spit in his mouth to lick the dirt off his cracked lips.

THEIR ONLY HOPE
September 3, 1862

Finally showing mercy, the late afternoon sun lowered itself toward the horizon. Johnny's back rested against a stack of dead animals and soldiers, wagon boxes, livery tack, and cook pots. A terrible stench permeated everything. The Indians kept firing into the bloated bodies of the dead. The gut and blood smells were so intense Johnny couldn't draw a deep breath without gagging.

Johnny swiped his arm across his eyes and started scraping at a bullet with his knife so it'd slip down his gun barrel. His head ached fit to kill him before the Indians could. He rammed a load of powder down his rifle and dropped in a lopsided ball, hoping it would not explode in his face. He wouldn't fire until he had a sure shot. They couldn't afford to waste bullets.

The Indians didn't seem to have any shortage of ammunition. Johnny stood and threw his blanket over the bloated dead horse to cover the sight. Smelling it was bad enough. He rested his rifle atop the rough wool-covered mound and searched the birches for a target.

Was that shooting he heard off to the east? It sounded like big guns, maybe cannons. Chaska heard it too; his head was cocked. Johnny stretched his neck out, trying to hear better. It was yelling and war cries and gunshots and cannon fire!

"Reinforcements!" yelled Johnny. "They're coming!" Shouts all along the line echoed, "Cannons! We're saved!"

Chaska barely reacted. "It's another battle. But it's not coming here." The edges of his face tightened, "They're not moving anywhere."

Joe bent toward Chaska. "I saw Chief Mankato take about thirty of his warriors east a while ago. I thought they dropped back for food and water."

"I reckon his scouts spotted the rescue force, and Mankato went out to head them off," said Chaska.

"But there's cannon fire," insisted Johnny. "It's probably Jones or Bishop's gun crew. They'll break through." He'd seen up close what cannons could do to an Indian charge.

The soldiers popped their heads up over barricades to watch their rescuers arrive, but enemy fire forced them to duck down. The battle here sure wasn't over.

Johnny started to whittle down another ball, so hard

he scraped his finger. He put his finger in his mouth and sucked at the oozing blood. The moisture felt good in his mouth. He wished he had some water. The troops would have some when they got here.

"Chaska? Are they any closer? Can you tell?"

Chaska gave his head a quick shake. "They're not moving. They're pinned down same as we are."

"But you can't pin down cannons. They should have blasted through by now." Johnny sucked his finger again. It tasted salty.

Chaska watched him licking. "Here, suck on these." He handed Johnny a couple of small pebbles. "It'll bring saliva to your mouth."

The sporadic exchange of gunfire resumed. More hours dragged by. It didn't seem as if help would come anytime soon. Johnny's hopes sank with the setting sun.

Joe nudged Johnny's arm. "Here, take a swallow," he said, handing Johnny the last, long-awaited water bucket. "One swallow per man."

Johnny cradled the bucket like it was a newborn babe and tipped it slowly and carefully against his mouth. It was so good, so good. He passed it on and licked his moistened lips, rubbing them against each other, sucking them inward to prevent the slightest evaporation.

A large orange moon rose in the east, gracing the

killing fields with just enough light to fix on a target. Dakota campfires flickered just beyond rifle range, and the aroma of roasting meat wafted out from the coulee and through the army bivouac. The Dakota had food. They had meat. And they had all the water they needed in the creek.

Joe nudged Johnny again. Johnny turned quickly. Was more water coming? Joe held out a cabbage. "It's all that's left. One leaf only." Joe chewed his wilted leaf into a wad that pouched out his cheek like chewing tobacco.

Johnny broke off a leaf at the base of the core, ripped an edge loose and tucked it into his mouth, bruising it slightly with his teeth to release its moisture. He had to force himself not to stuff the leaf in whole and gulp it down. Eating slowly, his mouth would enjoy it more than his stomach. His stomach could wait.

Captain Anderson darted over to their position, followed by a couple of men lugging armfuls of rifles. The captain handed an extra rifle to Joe, then to Johnny, then to Chaska. "Now everyone has two rifles. Keep the bayonets fixed and handy." With a reassuring pat on each shoulder, he moved on down the line.

Johnny turned the army rifle over in his hands. It was a new Springfield rifle, much better than his own. They sure could have used them earlier. He glanced at Chaska, puzzled.

Chaska's eyebrow arched ever so slightly. "They're from the dead soldiers."

Thundering hoofbeats approached, riveting everyone's attention on a lone brave galloping toward their camp, carrying a white flag in one hand and a feathered staff in the other. Silhouetted by the rising moon, sitting tall astride his painted warhorse, the brave raised eagle feathers to display his war prowess. "Soon we will sweep down on you like an owl upon helpless rabbits," the warrior called, his voice dripping arrogance. "But we do not wish to shoot anyone with Dakota blood. Send out the mixed-bloods to us. They will not be harmed."

Everyone looked at Captain Anderson, who in turn looked questioningly at Joe and Chaska. Johnny guessed he was giving them the option. Of course they wouldn't go. He was sure Chaska wouldn't leave. Or would he? Joe might go, though—to get to his little girls.

"I'm not going over!" Joe shouted to the captain. "After killing Traveling Hail's son, I'd be dog meat."

"They'd kill us all," said Chaska, staring curiously at Johnny's face.

There were seven others. "We'll all stay," said Iron Face.

One of the sergeants, equally arrogant as the messenger, hollered back, "Cowards! You fight like Chippewa. Go back to your squaws."

Grossly insulted, the brave pitched his white flag at them as if it were a lance and raced away. Firing on both sides broke out immediately and the rider's horse was shot out from under him. Infuriated Dakota intensified their shooting.

But no Dakota attack followed. Night, now cold as death itself, enclosed its arms around the camp as completely as the Dakota surrounded it. The moon seemed to dim, relinquishing only enough light so the soldiers could see to reload their rifles. Hours stretched out interminably, the groans of the wounded and dying mingled with their pleas for water. Johnny's tongue swelled; his throat parched. Grimly he reloaded and scanned the moonlit landscape.

Beside him, sighting for a target, Chaska asked, "Did you think I would go back?" His voice held no hint of anger, no sign of disappointment.

"I wondered," admitted Johnny. "We'll likely die here." He turned his cheek over the gunstock to look at Chaska. "I don't want you to die, if you might live. It's no dishonor to return to your father's people."

"I won't leave you," said Chaska. "To die here will be to die with honor. Beside my brother."

Johnny blinked a couple of times, wondering how eyes so dry could call up a tear. He turned back to the dark trees rimming the encampment. No one slept that long night, except the dead.

~~~

As the faintest tinge of light pinked in the east, Captain Anderson made his rounds.

"Be ready," he said. "I expect an attack at dawn. Hold your fire till my order."

As sunlight spilled over the horizon, the prairie erupted with galloping ponies, charging braves, and screaming war whoops. Arrows, bullets, tomahawks, and lances flew at the soldiers' defensive line.

Johnny's heart stuck in his swollen throat. The attacking braves drew closer; vengeance pouring out of their hearts and mouths, they fired steadily into the compound.

"Fire!" yelled Captain Anderson. Gunfire and smoke cascaded over the breastworks into the charge.

Johnny fired first one rifle, then the other, at the braves racing toward the compound. He reached into his bag for more whittled bullets. It was empty.

"Just fire powder," said Chaska, sighting on his targeted enemy. "They won't realize our bullets are gone."

Johnny's glance darted around the compound; he saw others reloading. Return fire would still be effective.

Exhaustion forgotten, every able-bodied man fought back fiercely, their officers shouting encouragement.

Volley after volley met the charging warriors until finally they broke off their attack. Their charge collapsed. The battle returned to a deadly exchange of gunfire.

"Surely help will come today," Johnny said to Chaska, whose only response was a slight shrug.

About mid-morning, Joe yelled hoarsely, "There's a warrior riding in from the northeast! He's heading for the coulee!" They could all hear the painted brave's shouting as he galloped into the Dakota's ravine campsite.

"What's he saying?" Captain Anderson called. "Can you hear?"

Joe listened a minute. "He's warning them that the white soldiers are coming!" he hollered, voice raising a notch. "The scout says there are 'three miles of white men!'" Everyone held his fire and listened. Distant cannon fire rumbled again.

"It's getting closer," yelled Chaska. All along the line men listened with relief. The enemy fire petered out. In small groups, in larger groups, amid shouts and hollers, the Dakota withdrew. The warriors galloped past the soldiers' barricades, sending a final shot or arrow into the compound. Screeching wagon wheels lumbered out of the coulee and away, the Indian women urging their horses to pull harder and move faster.

Exhausted, Johnny slid down and leaned back. Soldiers all but collapsed in their dugouts and waited for help to arrive. They waited for hours. Johnny looked into the blinding sun, wondering if it had stopped its course across the sky. He stared back down at the flapping white canvas cover of Dr. Daniels's wagon. Torn edges and ripped sections flapped and snapped in the hot wind. There was no one moving anywhere, no sounds except wind and dying men's groans. The bright sun grew hotter, scorching eyes and skin. Crows circled overhead, flapped down beside the dead animals and pulled at them. Sounds of flapping, snapping, and cawing filled Johnny's ears. The bright hot sun beat down against his seared eyes. His mouth and tongue and throat were parched.

"Hello, the wagons!" Finally, voices shouted from close by. Johnny struggled to his feet along with the others. Chaska waved his rifle, signaling the relief troops to enter. After pulling down a section of barricade, mounted soldiers rode into the nearly destroyed bivouac.

The horses shied and snorted, their riders stared wide-eyed and open-mouthed around the area. Quickly they pulled their neckerchiefs over their noses and mouths, but their eyes betrayed their horror.

At first puzzled, Johnny looked where the soldiers

stared. He saw overturned wagons, broken apart and splintered. There were scattered heaps of equipment and supplies. And stacked bodies—of horses and men. The terrible stench was overwhelming. The injured men, wound with bloody bandages, raised their heads and cried for water. The men still at their posts staggered forward, faces peeling from sunburn, lips cracked and seeping blood.

Snapping to action, the rescuers grabbed their water buckets and dippers and tended to the wounded. Bucket after bucket passed among all the survivors, and soldiers braved a trip to the coulee to refill them from the creek. Makeshift blanket-and-pole stretchers transferred the wounded into the relief wagons.

Johnny, mouth dripping from a deep plunge into a water bucket, looked up and saw Dr. Daniels climb into the wagon sheltering Mrs. Krieger. The canvas was laced with bullet holes; splintered and tattered, spokes shot out of the wagon wheels. Dr. Daniels came out smiling. "She's alive. A bullet grazed her wrist. She'll be fine."

Near Johnny, a young soldier who had fought alongside Dennis reached into his breast pocket and pulled out a small Bible. A faint smile traced his lips as he paged it open. "Stopped a bullet," he said, inspecting the hole through the front cover. "It went through

Genesis, Exodus, Leviticus, and Numbers, but got stopped by Deuteronomy."

Dennis attempted a weak grin. "Never made it through Deuteronomy myself."

With food and water inside them, the men rested, watching a burial squad dig a mass grave. Respectfully the fallen soldiers were wrapped in blankets and lowered into the ground with dignity. When the dirt was finally filled over, shovels tapped it smooth across a large mound. The entire company gathered around, helping the day's survivors stand at attention as the bugler played taps, sadly, mournfully.

Tears ran down Johnny's face, washing a muddy streak through the caked dirt.

The last gunfire of the day was a salute to their fallen comrades.

CAMP RELEASE
September 25 and 26, 1862

Johnny poked a branch into the campfire, whooshing a shower of sparks and embers into the cold night air. Watching without comment, Chaska, Other Day, and Joe lay on the trampled prairie grass surrounding the sputtering campfire, sprawled against logs and army saddles. Brilliant stars in the black sky promised the first fall frost.

Scampering notes from a mouth organ caught Johnny's ear and he glanced across the encampment. Campfires cast dancing shadows on the canvas tents arranged in orderly military rows. A guitar twanged in with the melody, and soldiers softly sang, "Mine eyes have seen the glory of the coming of the Lord. . . ."

Johnny shoved another stick into the flames, stirring up spitting sparks. "Colonel Sibley is so slow! We would still be at Fort Ridgely if General Pope hadn't finally ordered him to move out." He straightened up and stared at the dark prairie. The sweet smell of dry clover wafted into the encampment. Somewhere out there, Amy was still captive. And Sibley had stopped and encamped!

"Sibley has his reasons." Other Day pulled a smoldering twig from the edge of the fire and held it over the carved bowl of his red clay pipe, drawing on the stem. "It would be foolish to move into hostile territory without troops and supplies."

Johnny squatted down on his heels and tormented the fire, the tip of his stick now burning. "The newspapers call Sibley 'the undertaker'. They say all his troops do is go out on burial details after the Indians have left." His eyes reflected flames as he looked up at Other Day. "Colonel Sibley's never taken the offensive. Even with all the troops he had at Wood Lake, Little Crow had an ambush waiting for him. It's only blind luck a foraging party discovered it in time."

"Little Crow's defenses are weakening. The peace party becomes stronger, the war party more divided," said Chaska, chewing on a long stem of prairie grass.

Snorting, Johnny jammed a punishing poke into a stubborn ember. "Then why didn't Sibley pursue Little Crow after the Wood Lake battle? He just sat and watched them ride away."

Other Day leaned his arm back on his saddle and drew in a draft from his pipe. "Go after him how? On foot? Sibley's only got twenty-five horses left after the Birch Coulee battle." Twin streamers of smoke exhaled from his nostrils. "And he has a plan. Sibley left a note on the Birch Coulee battlefield for Little Crow, inviting him to meet and negotiate a peace. Stuck it into the ground on a split stake."

Johnny rocked back on his heels. "Peace? He thinks Little Crow will negotiate peace terms?"

Other Day nodded. "Two mixed-blood captives of Little Crow have been carrying messages back and forth. That's what's been taking all this time. Colonel Sibley had demanded the release of all captives before he'd even discuss peace terms. Little Crow refused. He probably figured he'd need them as hostages. He's keeping plenty of distance between himself and Sibley's troops."

"Then what in God's name is going to happen to the captives?" Johnny jumped up and pointed across the five hundred feet of prairie that separated them from Red Iron's peace camp.

Joe kept his eye on the flickering campfires in Red Iron's encampment. "What if Traveling Hail killed my daughters?"

"Red Iron and Wabasha have Little Crow's captives," said Other Day. "They rescued them while Little Crow was at the Wood Lake battle."

Johnny swiveled, nearly losing his balance. "All of them?" He knew he didn't want to go back to the fort without Amy. Ma was already at wit's end. Pa couldn't leave her alone.

"No, not all." Other Day refilled his pipe with kin-nickinnick and glanced up at Johnny. "We don't know who is there and who is not."

Chaska, lying with his feet toward the fire ring, shoved a teetering log chunk further into the fire with his boot. Flames flashed up, lighting the angled edges of his face. Johnny stared at him, at his tight mouth and frowning brow, and realized Chaska didn't know where his grandmother was, or Raven. Were they in the peace party camp? Or had Little Crow taken them into Dakota Territory? Silently they all watched the flames die down to embers. Johnny pulled his rough woolen blanket up over his shoulders and shut his eyes against the stars.

〰

Johnny flew up off the army cot, the bugle boy's reveille as shrill as a rooster in the hen coop. He stretched his arms and sniffed freshly ground coffee beans. Joe cranked the coffee grinder as Chaska tended a small fire crackling in the ring of stones. Johnny grabbed the spider skillet, set it over the campfire, and reached into his ration bag for a chunk of side pork.

Gripping the grinder, Joe jerked the handle around. "Sibley had better not order another dress parade. We didn't need one yesterday morning; we don't need none now."

Other Day trotted over to them from Sibley's tent and squatted beside the fire, chewing on his pipe stem.

"What's the order of the day?" Johnny flipped the skillet and caught the sizzling side pork. "Will we leave immediately for Red Iron's camp?"

Other Day shook his head. "Not right away. Colonel Sibley's urging any hostile Dakota still around to surrender to him. He told me, 'Haste is threatening. We must move with due deliberation.'"

Joe slammed the coffee grinder onto the ground and stomped it with his foot. Johnny stared at the small broken boards, at the metal handle sticking crookedly out of the dirt. The bitter coffee aroma mingled with the wood smoke sifting up into their faces.

"Then when?" asked Johnny. "Today or next week?"

"Today," replied Other Day evenly.

〰〰

Blinding sun bore down on the assembled troops. They were lined up in formation, looking spanking sharp in dress uniform and everyone on foot. Colonel Sibley, with his scout Other Day alongside him, raised his sword high and ordered the march. Bayonets glinted. Flags snapped in the brisk autumn breeze. Strutting drummer boys and fife players set the marching beat. Johnny's heart beat wildly. Beside him, Joe was nearly jumping out of his skin. Johnny closed his eyes. He prayed to God that Amy was waiting. And that she was safe and unharmed.

The Dakota camp fluttered with white flags affixed to every teepee, to wagon wheel spokes, to sticks and poles. Waving Indians welcomed them into their camp, parting to make a pathway for the marching troops. Johnny forced himself to keep step. Chaska pointed at a brave who had wrapped himself in an American flag, mounted on a black horse covered with a white blanket. "There's a smart man. Identifies himself as a friendly right off."

Scarcely listening, heart banging wildly in his chest, Johnny frantically scanned the encampment. He couldn't see anything but waving, grinning Indians. Where had the captives been held? They must have been kept inside the lodges. Joe was biting his lip, probably to keep from screaming out his daughters' names.

At a central clearing, Chiefs Red Iron, Wabasha, Taopi, and Little Paul, dressed in fringed and beaded leather and great trailing headdresses of eagle feathers, greeted Colonel Sibley. Little Paul took Sibley's outstretched hand. "With a clean hand I take your hand," he said. "It is a good work we do here today." They sat on the ground, indicating they would council together. Everyone else, Indian and white, settled themselves in a circle behind them.

Chaska motioned Johnny to sit beside him. "Ceremonies come first. All must be done according to tradition." Johnny sat cross-legged. He breathed in deep lungfuls of warm autumn air, hoping to still his anxiety. Beside him, Joe's fingers drummed against his crossed leg. Amy is here, Johnny told himself. She's near; she's safe. Each of the assembled chiefs made a solemn speech, assuring Sibley they had never made war on the whites, telling how they had risked their own lives to secure and protect the captives.

Sibley listened, nodding occasionally till they finished, then he stood. "Release the captives to me," he ordered. He faced the row of lodges, his right hand resting on the hilt of his sword.

Johnny jumped up. At a nod from Red Iron, the tent flaps opened and the captives streamed out. Johnny's feet suddenly rooted into the ground. How terrible the captives looked—tattered and half naked, some laughing hysterically, some fainting, some numb with shock, dazed and confused.

Johnny dashed into the milling mass of stumbling people. "Amy! Amy!" Forging forward in one direction, then another. He stopped and turned completely around, searching desperately.

Joe shoved past him, arms outstretched, calling, "Elizabeth! Minnie!"

Two little black-haired girls slammed into him, crying, "Papa, Papa."

Johnny sucked in gulps of air, swiveling around and around. Johnny spotted a blur of blue gingham. Struggling to him, blond braids loose and tangled, Amy pushed her way through the knots of people. Johnny scooped Amy into his arms, bear-hugging the breath out of her. She hugged back, gasping out words he couldn't understand because his heart beat too loudly in his ears.

Amy was back. She was whole and alive and in his arms. Thank God. Thank God. He rested his cheek against her hair, pushing back unwanted images of Clara Jones, of Emilie Paulie.

Amy clung to him. When finally her sobs gave way, she asked, "Ma? Pa? Are they all right?"

Johnny took several long deep breaths before he could answer. "Yes," he whispered. "Waiting for us back at Fort Ridgely." Unmoving, they held onto each other for a long time while their minds and souls calmed. The confusion and clamor around them gradually lessened.

Finally, an arm fell across Johnny's shoulder and he

heard Chaska say, "Time to leave."

Chaska. Had Chaska found Star Woman and Raven? He lifted his head, almost afraid to look.

Chaska was smiling, his face crinkling. Star Woman stood beside him, clutching a large woven basket. Raven carried a big wrapped hide bundle. "Time to leave," Chaska said again.

With an arm holding Amy close, Johnny walked alongside his friend and brother, who had his own arms around Star Woman and Raven. Late afternoon sunshine cast long slanting shadows that stretched eagerly ahead to the military encampment Sibley had named Camp Release.

CHANGE OF PLANS
Evening, September 26, 1862

Johnny dropped his armload of gathered firewood alongside the crackling campfire. Star Woman nodded her thanks as she broke the branches and twigs in small pieces and fed them to the flames, keeping her stew pot burbling.

Amy, on her knees alongside Star Woman, chopped and tossed chunks of potatoes, carrots, and onions into the black iron kettle. Johnny stooped over to sniff the steaming pot, grinning at Chaska and Joe seated on a log looking lean and hungry. Joe's girls looked liked they'd dive into the stew pot if their Papa allowed it.

Amy handed Johnny a carrot chunk. "I'll bet you're tired of eating hardtack and jerky. How about something more like to stick to your ribs?" She winked at Raven, who was scraping the inside of a rabbit hide.

Rabbit stew, Johnny figured. That'd do just fine.

"You have salt?" Raven tilted her head to look up at Johnny.

"I've got some," Chaska told her, inclining his head toward his saddlebags.

Raven trotted over to them, and Joe's little girls squealed and ran after her. Johnny raised his eyebrows questioningly at Chaska.

"They know Chaska has maple sugar in there too," said Joe. He pulled tin plates and cups from the kitbags and set them near the campfire. "I don't think they've had much to eat these past weeks."

Licking brown sugar from their fingers, the girls ran back to their papa and snuggled up on each side of him. "We didn't have good things to eat like Mama makes," chattered Elizabeth, tongue scouring the grooves in her palm.

Minnie twisted to look up into Joe's face. "Sometimes we got awful cold. We slept on the ground. We didn't even have a blanket." She tucked herself closer under her papa's arm. "We were so lonesome." Seeing Raven ladle stew into clay bowls, they squirmed out of Joe's grasp and bounded over to her, arms outstretched. Raven placed steaming bowls in their cupped hands and they scooped in with carved wooden spoons.

Amy filled the tin plates, handing Johnny a mess plate heaped so high that gravy seeped over its edge. Filling a plate for herself, Amy settled down against the log beside Johnny, both stretching their legs straight out. Stew steam floated straight up to Johnny's nose, making his mouth water. Between heaping spoonfuls, he smacked his lips, making "mmm" noises.

"Tell me true, Johnny," said Amy, wiping a little gravy trail off his chin. "Best supper you ever had?"

Spoon halfway to his mouth, Johnny stopped and looked around the circle. Everyone was watching him with big grins on their faces. He looked at Amy. She had the biggest grin of all. Shrugging, he shoveled the stew into his mouth. "Can't deny it," he mumbled through bulged cheeks. "Beats dead horse any day." He quickly pulled his plate aside when Amy pretended she would overturn it.

Perhaps drawn by their laughter, a little girl scampered over from the next campsite and climbed onto Amy's lap.

Johnny offered her a chunk of his cornbread. She was cute as the dickens, couldn't have been more than three years old. "Looks like you made a new friend in Little Crow's camp," he told Amy.

Amy brushed the child's hair back off her forehead. "She stayed in the teepee next to us. Her name's Nancy."

Cornbread crumbs dropped to her lap as the little girl looked up at Amy. "The Indians killed my papa on his birthday. We were going to have a good dinner.

Mama made a cake and everything nice and Papa came home with a load of hay and the Indians shot him." She took another bite of cornbread, words tumbling out with the crumbs. "But my papa isn't dead for sure. He's in heaven with God." She reached into her lap to pick up spare crumbs.

Johnny set his plate on the ground beside him, not hungry anymore.

Joe got up abruptly, taking both his girls' hands. "Come, the soldiers have molasses cookies." Nancy, still holding tightly to her cornbread, ran after Joe and his girls.

The next few minutes stretched out slow and quiet, till Johnny got up and poured himself a cup of coffee. "Did you have enough to eat when . . ." He stopped, looked from Amy to Star Woman. "Did all of you have food enough? Did you fare well?"

Were they well treated, is what he wanted to ask. Had they been abused in any way? Chaska shifted forward, ever so slightly. Johnny guessed he wanted to know too.

"We had enough to eat." Amy seemed to guess his unasked question, too, her voice softening. "Star Woman dressed me in buckskins and darkened my hair and skin with water in which she had boiled black walnuts. I walked about freely with Raven, and the Indians treated me well."

Amy stopped a moment, looking inward, remembering. "Sometimes, when the warriors returned from a battle defeated, their anger raged. Star Woman would hide me beneath buffalo skins inside the teepee." She flashed Star Woman a tender glance. "One time a brave wanted to buy me for his squaw. But Star Woman told him she would keep her daughter. That her daughter could do more work for her than the pony he offered."

Chaska's attention focused on Star Woman. "We suffered no harm," she murmured. "Bad times come upon all. People react as people do. Some are kind, some are not. Some are brave, some are not. Some wise, some not. They do as they need to do. Like all creatures of the Great Spirit."

Sudden sparks whooshed up into the air as a burning log collapsed in the campfire, illuminating Star Woman's face. "Like fire." She gazed into the flames, seeing far beyond them. "Fire warms us, cooks our food, hones our weapons, gives us light. Yet it can consume forests and prairies, kill animals and destroy villages." Flickering lights and shadows cavorted across the creases in Star Woman's face. "As the Great Spirit called it into being, fire also does what it needs to do. As do water and wind. So is the nature of all things and all beings that spring from our Mother Earth."

≈

"Johnny, rise up." Amy gently tugged his blanket. "Breakfast's ready."

Rising up on one shoulder, Johnny peered through early morning darkness at a thin sliver of pink on the eastern horizon. Chaska stirred beside him, his breath condensing in the sharp cold air. Star Woman, up before the bugle boy, leaned over a campfire that seemed too little to cook much breakfast. Johnny stood and brushed frost off his blanket. He didn't smell coffee boiling or bacon sizzling or biscuits baking.

Star Woman ladled porridge into bowls and handed them to Johnny and Chaska, who set themselves on the campsite log. Joe and his daughters got up too, the girls sleepily reaching for their hot steaming bowls. Shivering, Johnny draped his blanket over his shoulders then examined the contents of his bowl. It looked like white cornmeal.

"Milled oats." Amy sat next to him, spooning deep. "With dried currants. Hot and tasty. You'll like it."

He stirred his spoon around in the porridge. Tiny red berries surfaced. He watched the little girls; they seemed to like it. He gave it another stir. It seemed thick. "Is there any milk?" Reminded of milk, Johnny jerked sideways to look at Amy. "What happened to Bessie? Who has her now?"

Amy took a dainty hot spoonful in her mouth, swallowing quickly. "Old Bessie got clean away. I thought I had time to milk her in the stables before we went back to the fort, but that's when the Indians snuck in. They sure were taken with all Bessie's fresh milk. They almost got into a fight over who would get her." She licked oatmeal off the spoon edge.

"So what happened?" A slight edge hardened Johnny's voice. Everyone stopped eating, listening to Amy's story.

"Bessie settled the argument herself." Amy waved her spoon to show what happened where. "She kicked the Indian behind her, shoved the one beside her to the floor and stomped him with her front feet, then head-butted the one who grabbed her collar. I think she poked another one with her horns when she stampeded past him out the door." She laughed, pointing her spoon at the imaginary door. "I should have jumped on her back. She probably ran all the way to St. Paul."

"Did they get mad?"

"No, nobody wanted Bessie after all that." Amy grinned at Johnny. "I really do think we should call her 'Old Bossy'. If we ever find her again."

〰

Finishing their hasty meal, Johnny and Chaska threw saddles over their horses, Chaska again riding his pinto Lightfoot. "Other Day will have to stay with Colonel Sibley, won't he?" Johnny asked, fastening bedroll and saddlebag. Raven, attaching a travois to her horse's shoulders, straightened up, and looked at Chaska. "Who will get Aunt Becky from Hutchinson?"

Star Woman stopped tying bundles to the leather drag. "Other Day cannot go back to his farm? Is not the war over?"

"Not for me," said Joe, buckling the bridle on his horse's cheek. "I'm taking my girls to their mother, then I have to report back here. I'm signed on as a scout in the army." He pulled tight on the narrow leather strap. "If Sibley decides to pursue hostile Dakota, Other Day and I must go along. Maybe into Dakota Territory."

Chaska, finished with Lightfoot, helped Raven and Star Woman secure their few belongings to the travois, wrapping it tightly with rawhide strips. "I'll take you to our farm," he told them. "If the house is burned down, we'll erect your teepee. Then I'll go and get my mother." He shot Johnny a worried glance.

"We'll be close by," Johnny assured Star Woman. "If there's any trouble, from whites or hostile Indians, you'll come to our place."

Silhouetted by the rising sun, Other Day strode toward them, the fringes on his leather tunic flapping in rhythm with his strong arms and legs. Johnny couldn't see his face clearly, but there was anger in his stride. Was something wrong?

Other Day stopped face-to-face with Chaska and put his hand on his shoulder. Chaska, standing tall and straight as always, straightened another fraction of an inch. They stared at other, not saying anything. Johnny felt they knew each other's thoughts.

"You must stay," Other Day told Chaska. "It was reported to Colonel Sibley that you were seen beside Little Crow during the battle at Fort Ridgely. You will have to stand trial before the military court."

What to Do?

Late September—Mid-November 1862

The team broke from their steady trot into an awkward canter as they approached the farmstead, and Johnny gave them free rein. His stomach knotted up again— what would be left of their homestead?

"What if it's all burned to the ground?" Ma's voice trembled like yellowed birch leaves. "Is there time to build a cabin before winter comes storming down on us?" It heartened Johnny to see Ma thinking about the future, even if it was to worry. Worry sat on his own shoulders like a backpack on a mule. Rebuilding the cabin was only the beginning. They'd need a barn. They'd need forage for the horses and food for themselves, what with winter coming hard on their heels.

Light worries, those were, needing only hard work in a hurry. Heavier on Johnny's mind sat Chaska, detained at Sibley's camp. Hard work wouldn't set Chaska free. Johnny shifted his shoulders to settle worry's burdensome weight.

The horses cantered into the clearing, abruptly planting their heavy hooves in front of the charred foundation of their barn. They shook their heads at the lingering smell of smoke snaking up through the humpy gray ash pile. Ma scrambled off the wagon and ran toward the cabin, Amy hard behind her. They stopped as suddenly as the horses had, gawking up at charred log walls that canted slightly outward. Johnny and Pa walked around the cabin, surveying the damage top to bottom.

One hand shielding his eyes, Johnny pointed up at exposed rafters that hadn't entirely burned. "I reckon the fire started on the roof, burned partway through, and collapsed into the cabin. It must have rained—fire wouldn't have gone out otherwise."

Pa's gaze swept the gritty, ashy homestead. "The Indians didn't spend much time here, I'm thinking— just set things afire and kept going. The hay and straw piled in the loft fueled the barn fire." They walked around to the front of the cabin.

Oddly, the porch seemed unharmed; black-eyed Susans still blooming alongside. Ma, her hand leaning on the empty door frame, peered inside. "The fireplace looks workable." Her trembling-leaf voice pattered lower, like leaves falling.

Amy poked her head in past Ma's shoulder. "There's

lots of stuff still in there. It can all be set to right." Turning her back on the cabin, she stared at the ruined barn, shoulders slumping. "There's no barn, though, and no Bessie. And no milk."

Pa stepped onto the verandah, his weight testing its strength, his hand pushing tentatively against the tilted porch post. "Tether the horses where there's grass, Johnny. We'll get the cabin cleared out today and start repairs tomorrow. Maybe we'll get a new roof on in a couple of days." He stepped to a corner of the cabin to inspect the log joints, tapping charred chinking. "It appears sound. Fixable."

Johnny ran to get Pa's toolbox out of the wagon, hoping there were root crops still left in the garden. They hadn't time to spare for gathering foodstuffs, or for hunting.

〰

Johnny kicked the big workhorse with his heels, urging it to a reluctant canter, mindful that Pa had told him not to lose this horse too. It had taken nearly two weeks to make the cabin livable, build a lean-to alongside it for the horses, harvest what corn was salvageable and lay away a minimal food supply. Hauling his worry-load about Chaska all the while. Pa kept telling him that Other Day could handle things, but Johnny knew that Chaska needed him to be there. Truth be told, Johnny needed to be there for his own sake.

But first, he needed to see Chaska's mother Becky, to tell her what was happening. He rode to the house where Becky now stayed, too scared to leave her parents' house. He stepped onto the neat white porch and knocked on the door.

"Johnny!" Becky opened the door and pulled him inside. She hugged him as if her were her son too. "Has my husband sent news? How are he and Chaska faring?" She led him into the parlor.

"They are both well, and they send their love." Johnny took her hand. "Chaska is being held for trial. He was seen with Little Crow's forces at the Fort Ridgely battle."

Becky gasped, hand to chest. "It must be a mistake. He certainly had close ties with the village, but he would not have joined them in war."

"You're right, he hasn't," said Johnny. "But he and I were briefly held in Little Crow's village. I was freed, he was kept. And forced to ride with Little Crow till he escaped. Since then, he's been with me." He thought best not to tell her about the battle at Birch Coulee, she'd had enough bad news. "Other Day and I will get it straightened out."

"How are you faring?" Johnny asked. "Are you in any danger?"

"No, no," she said. "The folks here think I've left my husband. They're not very cordial, but they think I've 'come to my senses.'" She lowered her head, clasping her hands together. "The people here, and all through the state, for that matter, hold real bad feeling toward all Indians. And Indian sympathizers. All they know about are the attacks, and the hostages. They think every Indian in the state is out to kill them. They're scared to death."

She looked up at Johnny. "And not only here. Governor Ramsey, General Pope, and all the newspapers demand that every Indian in the state be hanged. Exterminated," she stammered, hardly able to talk for shaking. "What will happen to Chaska?"

"Chaska and Other Day are not worried; we all feel everything will be straightened out." Johnny stood, willing his voice not to tremble. "Trust your husband's efforts. As Colonel Sibley's scout, he has influence."

≈

Johnny tried to fit himself to the big horse's jouncing gait. His mind felt all a-jiggle with thoughts of Chaska. Of growing up with Chaska, of their families working together. Of all the wood lore Chaska had taught him, all the hunts they'd shared.

And all the terror they'd faced. Staring back at Death with an empty rifle forged bonds deeper than blood. And now he had to tell Chaska, and Other Day, that their own homestead had been destroyed with a vengeance. That nothing was left but bare parched dirt. He was glad Star Woman and Raven had decided to remain at Camp Release.

Johnny found the encampment all astir as he rode in, everyone packing their gear. Officers shouted orders, soldiers scurried around taking down tents and loading wagons. Johnny pulled up his horse and watched from a little rise. The adjacent Indian camp had spread out, grown larger since he'd left. He couldn't understand— why on earth would more Indians have come? Gloom hovered over their camp like a patient turkey vulture.

Finally he spotted Chaska's pinto, tied to a stake near an outlying teepee. Alongside, Star Woman and Raven packed their stuff on a travois hitched to their pony. Johnny rode over and slid off his horse's bare back, wishing he could as easily shrug off the pervading grimness. "Where's Chaska? With Other Day?"

Star Woman shook her head impatiently and busied herself tying a leather bundle onto the wooden frame-work with rawhide strips. Raven pulled Johnny a short distance away, not meeting his eyes, dropping more weight on Johnny's worry-load. She flung her arm at the scattered teepees, head tilting as though sighting an arrow. "All these Dakota surrendered to Sibley when he promised the innocent would not be harmed and those who participated in battles would receive a fair trial. Foolishly they believed the snake with forked tongue.

"The trials started the day you left. A mixed-breed named Godfrey was tried first. He was found guilty of murder in about ten minutes and condemned to hang." Her hard black eyes fixed on Johnny. "Then the military commission offered him a short prison term instead of hanging if he would testify about Indians he knew that had massacred whites."

Johnny flinched at her fury, knowing this development threatened Chaska. "What did he do?"

"Godfrey was willing to save his neck by placing others in a noose," spat out Raven. "He named warrior after warrior after warrior and told what they had done, when and where, as if he had witnessed everything. The commission pronounced them all guilty." Raven's voice wavered briefly, revealing fear. "He named Chaska as Little Crow's constant companion and said he'd taken part in the attacks on Fort Ridgely."

Unnerved by Raven's fright, Johnny focused on a lone scrub pine standing sentinel above dry dead prairie grass. "Did Other Day testify? Defend him?"

"Yes. But Chaska admitted he was at Fort Ridgely with Little Crow. As a hostage, not a warrior. He said he killed no one." Raven stared off into a willow copse as though spies and informants sheltered there. "Other Day spoke forcefully of how Chaska escaped Little Crow to fight alongside the whites, but the judges would not listen. Chaska's presence at the battle of Fort Ridgely was crime enough. He was pronounced guilty; imprisoned with all the others. Today they will move them all to the Lower Sioux Agency to finish the trials. Hundreds have yet to be tried." She looked up at Johnny, fury forsaken, her black eyes deep wells of fear. "Other Day could not save Chaska. Can you?"

Johnny rubbed his aching neck where the worry-yoke chafed, his glance sweeping the encampment. "Where's Chaska now?" Raven pointed to a fenced enclosure. "Keep my horse," Johnny called over his shoulder, running to the guarded fence gate. The sentry admitted him with an indifferent shrug and he stepped inside. Standing sullen and silent, imprisoned warriors watched Johnny approach.

Bracing his fear-shivery back, Johnny stood straighter, scanning the enclosure. There, at the far end, someone beckoned. Chaska! Johnny strode briskly through the wary crowd which grudgingly gave way. He grasped Chaska's hand, unsure if showing friendship might endanger Chaska among the other prisoners.

Chaska returned Johnny's grip eagerly. "It's good

you came today. Tomorrow we will all be moved to the Lower Agency. I want you to take Lightfoot." A faint smile played along his mouth. "He's restless here. He needs riding. Take him hunting."

Tremors rippled from Johnny's neck all down his back. Chaska wanted him to take Lightfoot? Had Chaska no hope of being freed? Had he been sentenced to life in prison?

With a slight shake of his head, Chaska said, "Take care of Lightfoot until I am free. Star Woman can't feed two horses, and Lightfoot would be stolen from her."

Shoulders slumping in relief, Johnny nodded. Chaska had read his thoughts, as always. "What else can I do?"

Chaska glanced nervously at prisoners who had sifted closer to hear their conversation. "Indian can no longer help Indian. You must seek help from white friends. Anyone who might have influence."

"What about Sibley? Can Other Day get help from him?"

"Sibley sways with the wind. White winds of hatred and revenge sweep across the land. Seek help from those who stand against it." Chaska's glance shifted to the encompassing fence that enclosed him more surely than the warriors that had surrounded Birch Coulee. "If there are any to be found." He looked down at his hand, still gripping Johnny's. "Then come to me again at the Lower Agency."

~~~

Time itself rides a swift horse, thought Johnny, riding Lightfoot back to see Chaska. He'd spent over two weeks talking to Reverend Riggs, to Dr. Williamson, to anyone of influence who might be sympathetic. But their speeches and editorials had accomplished nothing, moved no one. Terrorized for weeks, fear of any and every Indian in the state had consumed the entire white populace and they now clamored for revenge. Frustration gnawed constantly at Johnny—nothing he'd done had made any difference.

Cantering into the clearing at the Lower Agency, Johnny found soldiers were again breaking up their bivouac. A long line of oxcarts stood waiting outside the prison enclosure. What was going on? The teepee encampment was already deserted—where and why had the prisoners' families gone?

Tying Lightfoot to a low tree branch, Johnny entered the fenced prison camp. Directly inside stood Chaska and Other Day, heads bent, muttering fervently. Other Day wore a military jacket; evidently he was on scout duty. Johnny hesitated a second, then went up to them. Chaska grasped his hand, Other Day his shoulder. Tightly, desperately, scaring Johnny.

"What's happened?" he asked.

"The trials are over." Chaska's hooded eyes hid all thoughts and feelings. "Three hundred ninety-two Dakota have been tried, three hundred seven sentenced to death."

"Not you too? Condemned to hang?"

Chaska grimly nodded. Johnny nearly staggered; only Other Day's grip on his shoulder gave him the strength to stand.

"Sibley and Pope want the executions done immediately." Other Day's voice was as firm and strong as his resolve. "But they aren't sure they have the authority to execute so many. They wrote to the War Department in Washington for permission. That gives us time."

"Time may not matter." Chaska pointed to the guards, throwing the enclosure gates wide to admit soldiers brandishing bayoneted rifles. Like cowboys rounding up cattle, they shoved the prisoners toward the gate, shouting, "Form up! Hold out your hands to be shackled!" Like a wayward steer, Chaska was pushed into the milling herd.

Other Day moved close to the prisoner line, keeping his eyes on Chaska. Johnny followed, asking, "What does he mean—time won't matter? What could happen?"

"I just returned from accompanying the friendly

camp to Fort Snelling, where they will winter. Nearly seventeen hundred peaceful Dakota that never waged war, that protected white captives. Their caravan stretched out over four miles." He gave a fierce angry snort. "Going through Henderson, whites attacked us with knives, guns, clubs, stones. . . . It was all the guards could do to hold them off."

"The townsfolk attacked you? Was anyone hurt?"

Other Day stopped and turned to Johnny. "Old men and women and children were pulled off the wagons and beaten. A white woman tore an infant from its mother and slammed it to the ground. It died soon after." He gestured at the lines of Dakota warriors being herded toward the oxcarts. "Can you ride along to Mankato with this wagon train? To help protect these prisoners in case they're attacked too?" Around them, chains clanked, soldiers swore. Johnny nodded, not trusting his voice to speak.

"I will not be riding with you," said Other Day. "Star Woman, Raven, and other prisoners' family members will form a separate train. They will need protection as well, and Sibley has allowed his scouts to provide it. We will travel the back trails and meet you near Mankato. I'll take your horse; you take Lightfoot." Abruptly he strode to the prisoners' line where Chaska and three others, prodded by rifle butts and curses, climbed into a narrow wooden cart; they were shoved down and crowded together like animals sent to slaughter. The soldiers pushed the remaining shackled prisoners forward to the next oxcart. Other Day walked briskly up to Chaska's cart and clasped Chaska's arm. Johnny held back a moment, giving them what little privacy this cattle drive afforded.

Returning quickly, Other Day whispered sharply in Johnny's ear. "The danger is great—you'll pass New Ulm. Stay close to his cart."

Johnny ran to get Lightfoot, urgency prodding him as surely as the bayonets. New Ulm? Did Other Day think New Ulm citizens would attack the prison train?

Colonel Sibley led the procession. Standing in his stirrups, he brandished his sword. "Company, forward!" Wooden wheel hubs screeched against wooden axles, mules brayed, oxen bellowed, soldiers and drivers hollered orders to men and animals. The caravan staggered forward and out, surrounded by a full military escort waving bayoneted rifles on upright arms. Johnny hugged Chaska's wagon, shaken by the hatred and violence that whipped uncontrolled across the land like furious windstorms.

He held a tight rein on Lightfood, sure that the horse would bolt through this whirlwind were not Chaska alongside. He glanced at the oxcart he guarded. Chaska sat quiet, acknowledging neither his surroundings nor Johnny. Beside Chaska huddled two boys, maybe fifteen and sixteen. A fourth man had his head down on bent knees. Dust billowed around them; raucous noise engulfed them. Late fall sunlight slanted down, withholding its warmth. Jolting screeching miles rolled under them, stretching into long cold dusty hours.

Whenever they'd pass a white settler returned to his homestead, Johnny flinched as waves of hatred blew over them. The drivers sensed it too, whipping the plodding oxen.

Warnings sifted back from the lead wagons. "Look sharp. New Ulm's just ahead. Be ready for trouble." Guards muttered about having to defend Indian murderers against white settlers, and Johnny's anxiety mushroomed like cumulous clouds.

The caravan neared New Ulm's outskirts, its wooden wheels screeching their approach. Johnny peered through the hazy dust surrounding the wagon train. A large group of men worked in a field ahead. Were they harvesting? No, there were no hay wagons, no forage wagons. They looked to be digging. Potatoes? Big piles of lumber stacked alongside them. Were they digging a building foundation? "Chaska, stand up. What's that up yonder?"

Chaska stood, eyes narrowing in late afternoon

light. "Coffins. It's a burial party."

The settlers heard the squealing oxcarts. Pointing, gesturing, they were soon aware of what approached them. Screaming in fury, they stampeded toward the caravan, brandishing shovels and pickaxes. As though expecting a call to arms, more citizens mobbed out of New Ulm, armed with guns and knives and pitchforks, women with rolling pins and brooms, children with rocks and bricks. Attacking wolves, howling revenge.

Too late, oxcart drivers attempted to turn their carts as the crowd surged down on them. Mounted guards struggled to hold their horses as furious civilians darted between them, throwing rocks and brickbats, clubbing at anyone and everyone. Mindless of rearing hooves, two hulking farmers shoved into Lightfoot and dragged the two Indian boys off the oxcart, clubbing them with firewood chunks. A woman clad in black mourning dress screamed into their terrified faces, beating one boy, then the other, with her fists. Both boys covered their heads with shackled arms, leaving their bodies open to kicks and blows. A young boy whacked at them with a stick, his reddened face distorted with fury.

Johnny edged Lightfoot between the attackers and the cart, grabbing Chaska's arm and hoisting him up behind him. Seeing what Johnny was doing, the two farmers reached and grabbed at his legs, trying to get to

Chaska. The boy with the stick looked up, his face freckled with blood spattered from the Indians he had been beating on. "That's him!" he screamed, pointing at Chaska. "He killed my ma! My pa! That's him on the paint horse!" Whipping the stick over his head, ready to take out Johnny to get to Chaska, the boy rushed toward Lightfoot. Lightfoot reared, front hooves flailing. The oxen in the following cart staggered back, and Lightfoot, still up on his hind legs, stepped back through the gap they'd opened and dropped down. Front hooves hitting the ground, he darted through milling horses and people to the front of the line, Johnny and Chaska gripping his flanks tightly.

"Hold them off!" shouted an officer. Through dust and braying and screeching and hollering, the guards managed to form a defensive line, pushing people back and away with their horses' bodies. No shots were fired and no civilians were threatened, but with the soldiers crowding them, with bayonets nudging into them, the residents were forced to retreat. A surrounding row of armed guards held them back while remaining soldiers hoisted the beaten Indians back into the oxcarts and got the caravan moving again, protected by a rear guard. Furious curses flew at them, rocks hailed down on them, screaming wood wheel hubs seeming to give voice to everyone's fury.

Johnny hoped to ride near the front of the caravan, but an officer angrily waved him back. "Drop that Indian back in the oxcart," he ordered, pointing through roiling dust with his sword. Johnny slowly edged back, trying to find their cart. He looked for the two Indian boys. He thought he spotted the right cart. Without a word, Chaska slipped off Lightfoot's back into the oxcart and stood, bracing himself against its jolting sideboards.

The younger boy, his bleeding face looking like a slab of raw meat, cradled the bloody head of his older brother. Staring, Johnny realized the older brother was dead, his jaw obviously broken. Screeching wheel hubs beat against Johnny's ears like dying animals. He looked at Chaska, standing silent. Johnny had never felt so helpless, not in Little Crow's village, not in any battle.

Sibley had decided it was not safe to go into Mankato. He set up an armed bivouac at South Bend, and called it Camp Lincoln. He decided to wait there for the execution order to arrive from the president.

Other Day found Johnny there that night, standing under an aspen tree, armed and watching the road, quaking like the aspen leaves above him. Johnny went into his arms and Other Day held him. Slowly he drew strength from Other Day's silent resolve. Other Day had said they still had time. There must be things they could still do.

"The women's camp is set up nearby," said Other Day. "They are safe, for now. I must talk to Sibley. To make sure he has guards enough."

Johnny's fragile resolve started to unravel, remembering the unleashed fury at New Ulm. But Mankato hadn't been attacked—their citizens wouldn't retaliate. Would they? "What does Sibley need to guard against?"

"Lynch mobs," said Other Day.

WAITING ON THE PRESIDENT

December 1862

Fretful over the weeks that had passed, Johnny paced the long, elegant stone hallway of the Faribault Episcopal Church arching high above him. Bishop Henry Whipple was his last hope. His eloquent letters to the newspapers had pleaded for reason, for fair treatment toward the Indians. Would he take on Chaska's cause? Could Whipple's voice reach President Lincoln's ear?

The heavy oak door swung open and a tall gentleman, black-suited with a stiff white clerical collar, beckoned Johnny toward a tall high-backed chair. Easing into it, Johnny figured the president himself couldn't look more imposing than Bishop Whipple.

Striding behind his long dark desk like an Old Testament prophet on a mountaintop, Bishop Whipple sat with a flourish of black robe. "Tell me your concern."

First taking a deep breath, Johnny poured out Chaska's situation, taking care to present the facts calmly. It wouldn't do to look foolish before the dignified bishop.

Bishop Whipple listened intently, then said, "You will be heartened to know there are men in Washington who speak for the Indian cause. Commissioner of Indian Affairs William Dole protests the death sentences, saying it is unlawful to hang men who have laid down their arms and surrendered. Clergymen decry such a dreadful mass retribution. Statesmen call attention to our nation's justice as seen by Europe—how would massive killings appear to countries who have aided the Union cause?"

Johnny squirmed in the encircling chair as the prophet uttered chapter and verse. This was good news, outstanding news, but would it free Chaska? Would the bishop intervene on Chaska's behalf?

The bishop stood abruptly and turned to gaze out his tall windows at the wintry landscape. "I talked with President Lincoln myself; preached at him all the evils done to the Indians in the name of the American government and the Great White Father, till he felt it down to his boot soles." He turned back to Johnny, the congregation awaiting the Word. "But it all comes down to law. Lincoln requested all the trial transcripts, ordering his attorneys to present an analysis. Pray God he has the wisdom to discern guilt and innocence from such scanty records." He walked over to Johnny, shook his hand, and firmly ushered him out the door. "Pray God," he pronounced.

Riding Lightfoot back to Mankato, his bundled head bent against the icy north wind, Johnny's burden lifted ever so slightly with this mere sliver of hope.

〰〰

Winter winds and snowstorms prevented Johnny from traveling back and forth between his homestead and Mankato, so he stayed with Star Woman and Raven in their teepee. Other Day came every night for the evening meal, bringing news from military headquarters. Sibley had returned to St. Paul, head of the Minnesota Military District.

Bedding down Lightfoot and Raven's pony at the livery where he worked in exchange for boarding the horses, Johnny trudged through the snow to the teepee, carrying an armload of wood for the fire. Without the blankets and food sent by his family, he knew Star Woman and Raven would starve to death, if they didn't freeze first.

Johnny lifted the hide teepee flap, entered and stacked his log chunks. Raven tended a small stew pot suspended over the stone-ringed cook fire. A narrow trail of smoke swirled slowly upward, reluctant to leave the slight warmth of the teepee. Star Woman's face crinkled into a welcoming smile as she motioned him to sit on the buffalo robe spread on the ground. Raven, finding it harder to smile, ladled into the stew pot.

"Has Other Day arrived? Any news?" Johnny thought he'd go crazy waiting for news. He tried to tell himself the long wait was a good sign. If Lincoln had wanted all the condemned to hang, he'd have written so straightaway.

A whoosh of cold air whisked into the teepee with Other Day. Briefly greeting them, he quickly sat and ate his stew. Johnny hurried through his, too, keeping quiet.

Finished with his meal, Other Day sat back and filled his pipe with kinnickinnick bark. Pipe smoke swirled up in a little whirlwind. Between puffs, he spoke. "Colonel Miller received a dispatch from Washington this evening. He will read it publicly tomorrow, outside the prison." He glanced from Star Woman to Raven to Johnny, hesitating. "We must wait another night."

Star Woman settled herself onto the robe, taking the pipe from her son and drawing in a long breath. "Is there any news from Fort Snelling?"

Johnny knew she referred to the friendly camp that

wintered there. He shivered, knowing they had no extra firewood, no blankets. And that the army provided only bread and crackers.

Other Day nodded. "Many have died, either starved or frozen. And now, a white man's disease they call measles will take the rest. Hundreds will die before this winter is over." He took the pipe, drew in, and released bitter smoke, shrouding his face.

Star Woman got up and restacked the small wood-pile. Johnny watched her careful movements, aware she had concern for her own village as well—the Dakota who had fled with Little Crow into Dakota Territory. They'd had no opportunity to prepare a winter encampment, to stock up on food, to find a sheltered valley near a wood supply. A sudden wintry gust rattled the teepee canvas. No one spoke of Chaska, not wanting to put fear into words.

Johnny sat before the fire all night, staring into flames long after the others had burrowed under their buffalo robes. He was afraid to sleep. What if he dreamt of Chaska, facing a hangman's noose? He fed the fire till pale dawn slid down into the river valley.

〰〰

Soldiers rousted the prisoners out of the log building in which they had been confined after Camp Lincoln was deemed too hard to defend. Over three hundred shackled prisoners stumbled out into bright sunlight, shielding eyes that had grown accustomed to the dark sooty interior of the jail. Johnny, Other Day, a few town officials, and newspaper reporters had gathered in the snow-trampled courtyard as well.

Colonel Miller stood on a wood box and opened President Lincoln's official letter. The wind whipped at it, and he had to grip it top and bottom. Glancing from the paper to the huddled prisoners, he shouted out:

"Ordered that of the Indians and Half-breeds sentenced to be hanged by the Military Commission . . . you shall cause to be executed on Friday the nineteenth December, instant, the following:"

Scarcely able to draw breath, Johnny steeled himself as the names were read.

Colonel Miller, unfamiliar with Indian names, had no trouble pronouncing:

"Chaska."

Darkness crept around the edges of Johnny's vision; his hearing shut down. He rubbed his knuckles deep into his eyes, and from the central blackness, bright sun-yellow light radiated outward. Focusing attention on the light, he held onto consciousness. He didn't realize he was swaying till Other Day gripped his shoulder.

Other Day pulled Johnny's hands down, spoke quietly but forcefully near his ear. "You are needed. Collect your wits."

Johnny struggled to pull himself together; his blurry eyes focusing on Other Day's stern expression.

"Stay with Chaska. I'll find out what I can." Other Day turned abruptly and left.

Though he tried, Johnny couldn't get near Chaska. Crowding against a surrounding ring of soldiers, he saw Chaska separated from the larger group of prisoners like a calf cut out of the herd for branding. By the time the small group of condemned-to-hang prisoners was relocated, forced into a small stone building, Other Day had returned. The guard let them in to see Chaska.

Small windows admitted slight light into the single bare room and smoke from a woodstove dimmed it even more. Eyes adjusting to the scant light, Johnny spotted Chaska sitting on the floor, slumped with his head on his knees.

Other Day, voice firm and commanding, called Chaska's name. Chaska rose, straightened his back and calmly greeted his father, formally taking his hand, then Johnny's. "My father. My brother."

Other Day made no move to sit. Drawing the boys in close, he spoke in English.

"President Lincoln commuted the sentences of two hundred sixty-four of the condemned braves to prison terms, those who were judged only guilty of participating in battles. They are to be treated as prisoners of war."

Johnny's mind grasped for understanding. "Why wasn't Chaska included? There's no basis for hanging him!"

Other Day cleared his throat, ignoring Johnny's interruption. "He approved the execution of thirty-nine warriors, those who had been judged guilty of individual murders and atrocities against settlers." He stared into Chaska's and Johnny's faces. "A mistake has been made. They believe Chaska murdered someone." He focused attention on Johnny. "I will try to find out who accused Chaska. Colonel Miller said it would have to have been an eyewitness."

"But when? Where?" blurted Johnny. He glanced wildly from Chaska to Other Day. "No one could have seen such a thing." Sudden realization thudded against his chest. There were days when Chaska was unaccounted for; when no one could vouch for his whereabouts. How could Chaska prove he had not committed a murder?

"We must try to learn who is the witness." Other Day's voice was a hammer, pounding words into Johnny's ears. "But you must then find him; talk to him. Determine what he saw, and why he names Chaska. Convince him he is mistaken."

Johnny stared at Other Day, struggling to understand. Why him? How could he convince anyone?

Simply, quietly, Chaska explained. "What white survivor would listen to an Indian? Only you can help now."

〰️

Many hours and many questions later, Johnny galloped down the main street of New Ulm, pulled up short in front of Sheriff Roos's office and leapt off Lightfoot. He stopped only long enough to throw his blanket off his shoulders and over the pinto's lathered back and burst into the office. The sheriff and Jacob Nix rose quickly from the chairs they had pulled up to a parlor stove.

"Johnny Preuss, what brings you here?" Sheriff Roos's eyebrows drew together in a puzzled frown.

Johnny strode across the room, shaking their outstretched hands. "I need to find a witness. A boy who mistakenly named my friend as the warrior who killed his parents."

Sheriff Roos and Jacob Nix exchanged glances laced with suspicion. "There's lots of orphaned boys in this area. And lots of parents were brutally murdered. Whole families, in fact," said Jacob, stroking his handlebar mustache. "Is there any way you can narrow the possibilities?"

"I was riding guard with the prisoner caravan that went through New Ulm last month." Johnny determined to keep his tone reasonable. "To protect my friend, I pulled him onto my horse. A young boy pointed at Chaska and said he was the one who killed his ma and pa." He swallowed hard, but continued calmly. "Some of the soldiers saw what happened and reported it and Chaska is now condemned to hang. But he didn't do it. The boy accused the wrong person. I need to find him, to talk to him and find out why he thinks it was Chaska."

The sheriff rubbed his large hand through his hair, seeming to think things over, to sort things out in his mind. "I can take you to see a couple of boys who might have pointed him out. But to prove his innocence, your friend will have to have reliable witnesses who can swear he was elsewhere." He glanced at Jacob with questioning raised eyebrows.

"At a specified different place." Jacob seemed to have no problem with Johnny's request. "Can you swear to his whereabouts during the early days of the war? That would most likely be when it happened—that's when most settlements were attacked."

"No." Johnny was all too aware his voice had gone shaky. "Not every day."

"I thought not," muttered Sheriff Roos. "He sure

wasn't with you here when New Ulm was attacked." As though just remembering something, he grasped Johnny's jaw, turning his head. "How'd that bad cut heal? It's not real noticeable anymore, is it?"

Johnny stepped back, startled. He ran his hand down the side of his face and felt a definite raised scar. "I haven't given it any mind. It doesn't bother me none, except sometimes it itches." The familiar worry-load shifted on Johnny's back. How much help would he get from these men? Did they think justice meant hanging every Indian in the state?

"I know a few boys here in town who lost their parents," said Jacob. "Most likely we'll find the one who was there when the prisoner train went through."

Bundled into overcoats, the sheriff and Jacob accompanied Johnny to three different households that had taken in orphaned boys. None of the boys had been out at the prisoner train. Frustration built up in Johnny. If he couldn't find the boy in New Ulm, where else could he look? "Is that all there are?"

"There's a youngster staying at Dr. Weschcke's house," said Jacob.

It was near evening when they stomped snow off their boots on the Weschckes' front porch. Lantern light shone out through the parlor windows. A young towheaded boy opened the door, looked up at them and hollered back down the hallway, "Dr. Weschcke! Sheriff's here!" He stared curiously at Johnny.

Johnny stared back at him. This could be the boy. They stepped inside, taking care to stay on the rag rug.

Dr. and Mrs. Weschcke bustled into the foyer. "Come, come in," said the doctor, taking their wraps and draping them on the coat tree. Mrs. Weschcke poked her husband, tipping her head in Johnny's direction. "What? What's this?" sputtered the doctor. He peered through his spectacles, inspecting Johnny's face, turning his jaw to the lamplight. "Too much scar. It should have gotten stitched sooner." He frowned and his spectacles slipped down his nose. "Not your fault, not your fault. There's worse scars than that around."

Mrs. Weschcke brushed floury hands on her white apron, then gave Johnny a motherly hug. "On many a body and soul, scars are left." Her red-cheeked smile brightened the glow of the lamp. "Stay for supper. Mine dumplings feed both stomach and spirit."

An aroma of warm chicken gravy wafted through from the kitchen. Sheriff Roos's eyebrows lifted again, this time with delight. "As soon as we talk to the young lad. We can't send Johnny back home without dumplings to sustain his soul."

Much as Johnny's mouth watered for chicken and dumplings, he hungered more for information. While

Mrs. Weschcke stirred up more dough, the men and boys sat in the parlor. The youngster sat on a hassock, still looking curiously at Johnny.

"You've seen me before; do you remember?" Johnny asked him, thinking he couldn't be more than six or seven years old.

"Can't quite recollect," said the boy. "My name's Fritz. What's yours?"

"I'm John Preuss." Johnny pulled his captain's chair close to the boy. "Call me Johnny. You saw me on a pinto horse, the day the prisoner train went through here."

The boy jumped up, backing away from Johnny, eyes widened with fright. "The Indian was with you! The one who killed Ma and Pa!"

Dr. Weschcke pulled Fritz over onto his lap, gently stroking his back. "What do you need to know, Johnny?" asked the doctor. The friendliness in his voice seemed to make the boy realize he could trust Johnny. Fritz, thumb in his mouth, turned on the doctor's lap and watched Johnny.

"I need to know what day your parents were killed, and where it happened. Was it at your house? Where did you live?" Johnny spoke softly, smiling at Fritz.

Smoothing the boy's blond hair, Dr. Weschcke answered for him. "It happened August 28, the same day the Lower Sioux Agency was attacked. Before noon. Surviving neighbors brought him along when they fled here to New Ulm."

Relief flooded through Johnny like a rushing spring-time river. "Chaska was with his father at the Upper Agency that day," he spilled out. "They protected a large number of white people in the big stone ware-house that night."

The sheriff sat suddenly forward in his chair, look-ing sharply at Johnny. "I know about that. They were escorted north to safety the next day by an Indian named Other Day. He saved many lives, Other Day did."

"Chaska is the son of Other Day." Johnny gulped hard, nearly unable to continue.

Could this be the vindication Chaska needed? "All of those white refugees can testify that Chaska was with them that day and that night."

Jacob leaned back on the settee, seated beside the fireplace. Warm firelight lit his features, his bushy mus-tache casting a bushy shadow on his cheek. "It seems you now have your proof of time and place."

Johnny beckoned young Fritz over. "I took care of a boy about your age. His name is John Humphrey. I found him hiding in tall grass alongside a road after his family was all killed."

Fritz slid off Dr. Weschcke's lap and stood before Johnny. "Was there a big scary Indian all covered with war paint? On a big brown and white horse?"

Johnny put his hands on the boy's shoulders, gently, drawing him closer. "Young John didn't mention a brown and white horse. Fritz, are you sure it was a brown and white horse?"

Fritz's head bobbed up and down, blond bangs bouncing. "Yup, you couldn't hardly see it against the tree trunks except for those big white spots and . . ." He stopped talking, confusion creeping across his face. "It weren't no black and white horse, like I saw you on. It was brown and white," he whispered.

Except for the crackling of the fire, the room grew silent, listening. "You think, Fritz, maybe it wasn't the same Indian, either?" Johnny whispered back.

Slowly Fritz shook his head side to side. "I don't reckon it was. Now's I think on it, the Indian with you was smaller. Maybe he had lighter skin, too. And he didn't look near as fierce."

"You're sure on that, Fritz?" Johnny knew Sheriff Roos wasn't used to talking gently, but Johnny was glad to see that he was trying. "Think hard on what they both looked like. Were they one and the same?"

Fritz's face seemed to look inward as he concentrated, shuddering as resurrected memories flashed through his mind. He leaned into Johnny's arms, then looked up at him with wide blue eyes. "They weren't the same one. But the scary Indian—the one who really killed my ma and pa—is he going to hang? Did the soldiers catch him?"

Johnny tightened his arm around the boy. "I don't know, Fritz. Some were caught; but most got away. Maybe Dr. Weschcke could get information from Colonel Miller."

With a clatter of china, Mrs. Weschcke set a large steaming soup urn on the dining room table. "Come, eat," she called. With a scraping of chairs and flipping of napkins, everyone settled themselves around the table.

As Dr. Weschcke bowed his head and said grace, Johnny's heart spilled over with gratitude. He kept his head bowed a moment longer, silently thanking God for answered prayers. He added one more—that the governing powers recognize and acknowledge Chaska's innocence. That Chaska be truly spared.

EXECUTION
December 26, 1862

"Why would you want to go back there?" Johnny grabbed Chaska by the shoulders, shaking him as if he'd lost his wits. "You were released only yesterday!" Johnny had nearly taken leave of his own senses waiting for Chaska's official reprieve to go through all the proper channels. Finally, finally, Chaska had been freed from the prison. What on earth could he be thinking?

Chaska reached up and firmly unclasped Johnny's hands. "They die today. Do you think I would leave them now? That I would turn my back on my brothers?"

Johnny looked desperately at Other Day, seated by the cook fire, at Star Woman and Raven working alongside it. Not one returned his glance, tacitly agreeing with Chaska's decision. Sweat beaded on Johnny's face. "It's not safe for any Indian to be in Mankato today! Martial law has been declared; all the saloons are closed. The town is crowded with whites all eager to watch the hanging. And likely eager to do some lynching of their own. We should leave now." He swiped an arm across his brow. "We should have left yesterday."

Chaska lifted the flap of a leather bag slung over his shoulder, reached in and drew out owl feathers, small clay pots of blue and vermilion paint, kinnickinnick bark shavings, and red clay pipes. "My brothers need these things for their death songs and ceremonies. Come with me. When you see them, you will understand why it is necessary I do this." Chaska's eyes, deep black pools of grief, searched Johnny's for understanding.

Johnny faltered, his objections dissolving in those damp dark eyes. Chaska always knew how to reach Johnny, to give him what he needed. "You're right, Chaska. You need to go to them, and I need to go with you."

〜

Sun dogs flanked the winter sun, not yet high in the sky. The icy cold air froze Johnny's and Chaska's breath to frosty fog as they trudged to the jail, their boots scrunching noisily in the packed snow. The guard knew them and admitted them without comment.

As he stepped into the large windowless room, Johnny blinked several times, eyes adjusting to the dimness. Prisoners sat slump-shouldered on the floor; some lay huddled in blankets as if still asleep. Several were singing a Dakota hymn with the missionaries.

Chains clinked as the prisoners looked up to see who had entered. Startled, Johnny saw they wore leg irons, attached to bolts in the floor.

"To prevent war dances," Chaska muttered. He handed Johnny the tobacco packet and a handful of pipes. "Offer these around. I'll take the feathers and paint."

Johnny hunkered down beside an old man draped in a striped wool trading-post blanket. Through wrinkled folds of skin, the old man's black eyes squinted up at him. He motioned Johnny to fill the pipe and light it. Johnny did, drawing on the pipe and handing it to the old man, who drew deeply, releasing woodsy-smelling smoke in a long slow breath.

Chaska came and sat beside them, taking the pipe in turn. The old man rasped out Dakota words and Chaska translated: "Tazu says this: "'Tell my family not to mourn. I am old and would die soon anyway. I go to the home of the Great Spirit, and will always be happy there.'" The old man reached under his blanket and drew out a small pair of finely worked moccasins. "'I made these for my granddaughter. She was taken to Fort Snelling with my wife and daughter.'"

Tazu took the pipe from Chaska, chains softly clink-ing. He drew in another long slow breath and passed it to Johnny. Again, Chaska translated Tazu's words. "'Yesterday, soldiers from Fort Snelling brought farewell messages from our families. I learned my granddaughter had died of measles.'" His wrinkled, leathery hands fingered the fine needlework of the moccasins, traced the delicate lacing. "'I will see her today, in the next world. But I cannot take these along.'" He set them in Johnny's lap. "'Perhaps you know a small girl who would like them.'"

Handing the pipe to Chaska, Johnny turned the small deerskin slippers in his hands, Tazu's final loving gift, and no one to give it to.

Chaska took a long slow pull on the pipe, the wafting smoke dispensing ceremonial blessing. He returned it to the old man whose bent gray head was now shrouded in slow swirling smoke. Standing, Chaska tapped Johnny's shoulder, motioning him to follow.

They headed toward a tall, dignified warrior leaning against the wall, obviously aware of everything happening around him. Even in chains, his bearing was proud and regal as they approached. Opening his bag, Chaska withdrew bright white owl feathers, presenting them to the chief.

Tightlipped, with a curt nod, the chief also took paint pots and a small mirror from Chaska. With a quick, sure motion, he sat himself on the floor and daubed long blue lines down the side of his face, muttering in Dakota as Chaska sat beside him.

"Get paper and pen and ink from the guard," Chaska told Johnny. "Chief Rdainyanka wants to dictate a letter to his father-in-law Chief Wabasha."

When Johnny returned, Rdainyanka had finished painting his face and was nimbly weaving the feathers into his long black braids. Kneeling, Johnny spread the paper on an overturned wood box and set a squat black ink bottle alongside it. Dipping the crow quill pen in the ink, he scratched out the chief's words as Chaska translated.

"I have not killed, wounded, or injured a white man, or any white persons. I have not participated in the plunder of their property; and yet today I am set apart for execution . . . while men who are guilty will remain in prison. My wife is your daughter, my children are your grandchildren. I leave them all in your care and under your protection. . . . Let them not grieve for me. Let them remember that the brave should be prepared to meet death, and I will do as becomes a Dakota."

Chaska scrolled the paper and put it into his bag, saying a few words to the chief, who tersely nodded. The priest approached, but Rdainyanka waved him away. There was no medicine man, no holy man, present in the prison.

Tazu suddenly stood, shaking his blanket and tying it over his shoulders. As one, many condemned men rose with him, chains jangling noisily as they struggled to form a circle. The old man raised his arms overhead, his face lifting to the roof as if it were a sun-drenched sky. His thin wavering voice chanted, growing in strength as others joined in.

Rhythmic, haunting, mournful voices sprang up like a sudden spring rainstorm blowing across the prairie. Louder, stronger, wild and unearthly, the warriors' passionate song reverberated through the cold smoke-layered air, shimmering it into cirrus layers.

Chills ran down Johnny's back, goose flesh rose on his arms, the haunting chant compelling him to sway with it. Beside him, Chaska's arms raised, his body weaving like prairie grass, his voice prairie wind. Dark prison walls seemed to fade and disappear. Smoke became cloud and swirled around the warriors. Scents of air and grass and water wove with song and prayer.

Abruptly it stopped. At once, as one, every face, every muscle on every body, stilled to sudden silence. Johnny gasped in air, realizing he'd held his breath during the chant. Everyone yet stared at the dusty wood ceiling, wonder in their expression, gazing into the world beyond. Arms slowly dropped, eyes lowered as they returned to earth, to prison, to chains.

Rusty hinges squealed, wooden doors battered open against rough walls, and the soldiers entered carrying keys and ropes and white hoods and yet more chains. Removing the padlocks from the prisoners' leg irons, they pulled the length of chain through the floor bolts with clang and clatter. Next they bound the prisoners' wrists in front of them with rope cords. Stoically compliant, not one objected.

Not until the rolled-up hoods were placed on their heads, like caps. Many drew back in horror, grimacing, struggling away from the white cloths.

Chaska's fist clenched, his jaw tightened. "The hoods humiliate them. It is dishonorable to hide your face from death."

But it was done. The officer in charge swung open the door, glaring at Johnny and Chaska and the missionaries. "Visitors, out!"

Chaska and Johnny stepped out into cold bracing air, into blinding bright sunlight. Heads down, not speaking, they walked to the buckboard where Pa and Other Day waited alongside the frozen river that bordered the northeastern side of the town square. No one spoke as they climbed into the wagon, everyone's despair contained by desperate silence.

The wind quieted a bit, but still Johnny shivered. Standing in the wagon box, coat huddled against his neck, he viewed the entire square. Packed tightly, hundreds of milling spectators filled the streets, hung out windows of facing buildings, and perched on rooftops. Gathering his nerve, Johnny stared at the newly constructed gallows.

An enormous structure had been built of heavy oak timbers, about twenty feet high. The platform with the drop was more than seven feet off the ground. Beams across the top were notched to support forty rope nooses, which swayed and twisted in the wintry wind. Johnny swallowed hard, chilled to his soul.

Rolling drumbeats thrummed through the winter air, and ranks of soldiers marched into the square in precise military formation. The spectators fell back as two by two, a row of soldiers formed around the entire gallows, turned sharply and stood shoulder to shoulder, at arms. Following in close order, the next rank of soldiers formed another row ten feet outward from the first, this a double row, soldiers back to back facing the gallows and facing the crowd. They marched in place to the beat of drums, constantly thrumming drums, like hearts that would beat forever. The cavalry followed, hoofbeats in time with drumbeats, forming a row of mounted soldiers also facing the gallows. Smartly, swords were drawn and raised, their metallic swish a counterpoint to the relentless thrumming.

Lastly, two rows of soldiers formed a cordon from the jail to the gallows stairway. Perfectly in step, marching to the beat. They halted, each line turning to center, clicking their heels and standing at attention.

Suddenly the drums fell silent. Hollow empty silence, as if Death had entered the scene. Icy shudders ran through Johnny. He couldn't take his eyes off the jail door, flanked by armed guards. The provost marshal shattered the stillness, swinging wide the door and shouting, "Prisoners, out!"

Tall and straight and proud, the Dakota entered the bright sunlight glinting off fresh white snow, off reflective icicles poised like spent spears, off sharp steel sword blades. No one hesitated; no one balked. With dignity matching the soldiers', they marched single file through the lines of soldiers to the gallows and mounted the steps. Ushered into place by the execution detail, they each stood before a twisted rope noose that dangled and danced in their face.

As stone-faced soldiers lowered the white hoods down over their heads, the Dakota began their final death chant. Mournful discordant voices pierced the wary watchful square and flowed into the sky and the nearby river. An eagle overhead screeched, as if he would sing with them. Reaching blindly, twisting to grasp another's hands, the warriors called out their own names and those of others. Song and shouts and prayers mingled and swirled into wind and cloud and sky.

Johnny pulled his coat tighter around himself, trying to contain uncontrollable shivers and shakes. A slow measured drumbeat began and ended, perfectly timed. Then again, louder this time. And a third time, still louder. Like one of the condemned, Chaska grasped for Johnny's hand as though their own lives were forfeit.

Underneath the platform, a civilian in a heavy overcoat raised his arms high. Long strong fingers threaded around the thick wood hilt of a long blade. All the harsh beams of sunlight that pierced the bright sky focused on the sharpened steel knife, splitting into prism blades that struck at every watcher's eye.

Vengeance rippled through the executioner's arms. With a long loud "Haaahhhh!" he brought the long knife down on the single angled rope that supported the trapdoors. The rope frayed, strands whipping loose. Wham! Again the knife struck, an ax felling an ancient oak.

The trapdoors dropped with resounding thuds that slammed through icy air. Ropes jerked with the sudden weight as thirty-eight Dakota dropped to their deaths.

Deathly cold silence froze the town, and the moment.

From that brief stillness, a long low sound rose from

all around the square. Not loud; not a cheer—a throaty rumble like vengeance taken voice. Then silence reclaimed the air.

One rope broke loose and a body thudded to the ground. Nearby soldiers broke rank, scrambling to retrieve the body, scuttling back up the gallows steps with it. Propping it upright, pulling a spare noose over the flopping white-hooded head, releasing it to dangle through the trapdoor hole.

Everyone waited, eyes fixed, mouths agape. Minute after silent minute. Johnny almost wished for the drums again. Silence gave space for Death to gather his victims at his leisure.

Finally, the army physicians climbed the stairs to the platform. Walking from swinging body to swinging body, they put head to swaying chest, listening for heartbeats. They lifted hoods, looking for breathing nostrils, for a thread of life in bulging eyes.

As each Indian was pronounced dead, soldiers sliced a knife through the rope that held him, dropping him into another soldier's arms. Each detail carefully awaiting the next, the bodies were carried down beneath the platform and loaded onto army wagons pulled by mules.

"Where are they taking them?" Chaska had let go of Johnny's hand and wrapped his arms around himself, holding himself together as if his spirit might leave his body, as if he might not yet have escaped destiny.

"They'll be buried down by the river," said Other Day.

Johnny turned his head against the wind that had sprung up again. Snowflakes scattered across the square. Mumbling and muttering, the crowd began to disperse. From a few feet behind Pa's wagon, an old woman's strident voice cried out for unanswered justice. "And where is Little Crow? Or the braves that murdered settlers?" Quickly drained of anger, her wail crumpled into sobs of grief. "How many guilty will never have to account for the blood on their hands?"

Aghast, Johnny turned to the couple, bundled in blankets in their sleigh. "Some of these who died today were completely innocent."

Bitter anger screeched through the old man's harsh voice. "So were my children and grandchildren. Innocent! Every woman and child brutally massacred was innocent!" Fiercely he jerked his horse's reins, turning them into the wind.

Pa flipped the reins across his horses' backs with a sharp snap. Johnny and Chaska sat, backs against the wagon seat. Eyes slitted against harsh sun glare, they watched the gallows gradually diminish as they retreated from yet another killing ground.

CROSSWINDS

April 21, 1863

Brilliant April sunrise chased the ground fog into hasty retreat. Amy, snuggled for warmth between Johnny and Chaska behind the buckboard wagon seat, suddenly popped up into a splash of sunlight. "I get to choose the cow I want, don't I, Pa?"

Johnny tugged her sleeve, pulling her back. "No, Pa, don't let her. She can't tell a cow from a bull. She'll just pick whichever one has the biggest brown eyes."

Amy jerked back, glaring into Johnny's grinning face. "Pa, Johnny gets to choose his horse. I should get to choose my cow."

Pa exchanged a smile with Other Day, seated beside him on the wagon seat. "Provided the animal's sound," Pa agreed. An enterprising liveryman had rounded up livestock that had run free all winter from deserted farms and settlements where no one lived anymore. If they weren't claimed by today, they would go up for sale. Chaska and Other Day meant to buy a horse for

Johnny, a gift of friendship and appreciation. Other Day also wanted a team of workhorses and Pa aimed to find a cow to replace Old Bessie.

They had all started the day in fine spirits; the springtime air as fresh as just-washed linens on a clothesline. Approaching Mankato, Pa drove toward the common pasture down by the river.

The pasture fence had been raised and extended. Inside it, all kinds of farm animals jostled noisily for the first early sprigs of grass. Pa tied his team and wagon at a nearby hitching rail and they all walked over to the tall fence.

Amy stopped, hands on hips. "Maybe . . ." She scampered to the top rail and yelled down into the milling animals, "Here, Bess! Here, Bess! Come, Bess!"

An answering bellow resounded through the entire town square. Shoving and butting, Old Bessie pushed her way through the startled herd, nearly causing a stampede. Amy jumped over the rail and disappeared among hides and hooves and horns.

"Amy, don't go in there!" Johnny bounded to the top of the fence, ready to leap into the scramble. But once up there, he saw a wide area had opened around Old Bessie. She glared the other animals away, protecting Amy, who was hugging her neck. Johnny set himself on the top rail, grinning.

"Seems that's the cow she wants," said Chaska, who had followed him up the fence. With a warning snort, Bessie lowered her head and shook it every which way, displaying her horns and her intentions. She nearly tossed Amy too, but Amy knew Bessie's manner of speaking and hung tightly to her neck.

"Is that her cow?" squeaked a young voice. Startled, Johnny turned. A little girl had scrambled up and sat beside him.

"Where did you come from?" Johnny looked over his shoulder down at the gathered crowd. "Where are your parents?"

"My papa's down by the levee and Mama's at home." Leaning backward, she peered around Johnny. "Hello, Chaska. I'm glad you didn't get hanged."

Johnny nearly fell into the pasture himself when Chaska said, "Hello, Emma. I'm glad too." Johnny swiveled around, staring open-mouthed at Chaska.

A smile twitched the corners of Chaska's mouth. "Emma's pa is a newspaper reporter. He visited us in jail, and Emma would come along."

"Let's get her down off this fence." Johnny climbed down, hoping Emma would follow. She did, and Johnny lifted her off the bottom rail, avoiding a mud puddle. She sure didn't weigh much—little as a minute. Setting her on a grassy tuft, Johnny reached into the kit bag over his shoulder and brought out the moccasins Tazu had given him. Moccasins he'd felt he needed to carry till he found a little girl. "Would you like . . ."

With a little squeal, Emma grabbed them, plunked herself down on the ground and struggled with the buttons on her high-top shoes.

"Not yet," said Johnny, taking her hand and hoisting her back on her feet. "Take them home. It's too muddy to wear them now."

Clutching the soft leather moccasins to her chest, Emma dashed off up the street. Johnny didn't quite trust himself to speak, or look at Chaska. He was glad, though, that those sad deerskin slippers had found a little girl.

He and Chaska joined Pa and Other Day beside the rail fence and watched Amy maneuver Bessie through the milling crowd of animals.

"I guess you intend to claim that cow," said the liveryman, walking up beside Pa. He spit a long stream of tobacco juice into the mud.

Pa watched Amy cajole Bessie toward the gate. "I can't rightly say I'm glad to have found that ornery cow, but I reckon my daughter wants her back."

"She's welcome to her," said the liveryman. "I've been trying to get shed of that critter all winter. Everyone brings her back."

Chaska nudged Johnny and walked around toward a group of horses at the far side of the pasture. Johnny followed; they climbed the fence. Chaska pointed out a regal black stallion, half a hand taller than the surrounding bays, surveying the corral like he was king of the herd.

Intrigued, Johnny looked closer. A streak of white hair traced over its shoulder, trickling down the left front leg. An extraordinary paint. The horse rippled his shoulder muscles and the white streak seemed to flow like a spring waterfall over black stones.

"He was Rdainyanka's horse," said Chaska.

Johnny watched, spellbound. Who could be worthy of such a fine chief's horse? Chaska slipped down inside the corral, motioning Johnny to follow.

The other horses parted as Chaska walked through, Johnny close behind. Chaska approached the paint horse and held out his hand. The stallion nuzzled it and Chaska beckoned Johnny. "Come, meet Split Rock. Speak to him."

Johnny advanced softly. The paint pricked his ears forward, appraising him.

Stepping closer, he put his black velvet nose in Johnny's outstretched palm, snorting warm damp breath in it. Split Rock nickered softly, nosing first Johnny, then Chaska. Johnny glanced at Chaska, at the finally rekindled joy in Chaska's eyes. Was he going to claim the horse? A big lump rose in his throat.

"You can take that one out, if you can handle him," muttered the liveryman, spitting through the rail fence. Johnny turned. Was that man everywhere at once? Pa and Other Day stood beside him, and Other Day beckoned them out with tilted head.

The liveryman busied himself counting bills. "You got yourself a bargain," he told Other Day. "No one here can handle an Indian horse. Reckon he only understands Sioux."

Exchanging a private glance with Johnny, Chaska slipped a rawhide strip around Split Rock's neck and led Split Rock out of the corral. They walked back to the buckboard where Amy'd tied Old Bessie beside Lightfoot. Bessie wasn't sharing Amy's enthusiasm for her new halter.

Spotting them, Amy ran right up to the big paint, cooing and petting him as Chaska replaced the rawhide with a bridle. Johnny stroked the great horse's neck, moving his hand down the warm length between neck and mane, breathing in horse smell, alive and strong and free.

Other Day put his arm across Johnny's shoulder as Chaska lifted Johnny's hand, placed the bridle reins in his palm and folded his fingers around them. Johnny's eyes blurred and his breath ran ragged. This was too great a gift. With an impatient snort, Split Rock shoved his head against Johnny's chest, ready to leave. Everyone laughed, eager to dispel their overwhelming emotions.

Wheeet! screamed a whistle. Split Rock snorted, prancing sideways. Shouts rang out from all over the square; people ran to the levee. Johnny and Chaska steadied Split Rock, hastily tied him alongside Lightfoot and Bessie, and headed toward the river.

"A paddle wheeler!" Johnny ran down the slope to the levee. "It's steaming into the docking. The river must be open to St. Paul."

Loud steady drum rolls and the determined stamp of marching boots brought everyone to a sudden terrified halt. Johnny's heart chilled as he stood in the square, drumbeats throbbing in his ears, jerked back to that terrible cold December day. He turned, dreading what he might see. Stepping sharply, military troops cleared the street, heading to the levee.

"What's going on?" Johnny asked Chaska, standing behind him. Chaska shrugged, jaws clamped tight.

"Company, halt!" ordered the sergeant, and with a slap of gunstock and clap of heels, the soldiers formed into two lines on each side of the street. A cordon? For what?

"They're moving the rest of the prisoners out today," said a familiar voice behind them. Hands dropped friendlylike on their shoulders. "On the steamboat." Startled, Johnny and Chaska both swiveled around.

"Joe Coursolle," Johnny croaked, eyeing Joe's unique army uniform. "Are you still soldiering? What's this all about?"

Joe had embellished his blue uniform coat with a red sash, careful not to cover any of the brass buttons. He grinned at them from under his battered voyageur's cap, brushing dust off his sleeves. "I'm still a scout. Seems I enlisted for the full term." He pointed to the steamboat, dockworkers scurrying with ropes, securing it to the levee. "The governor intends to clear the state of Indians this spring."

Several Indian women scuttled down the street, struggling with bundles. The cordon led right up to the gangway, and the women boarded quickly.

"Those are the women from the camp where Raven and Star Woman stayed, here in town," noted Chaska. After a tense pause, a group of about fifty men trotted through the line and onto the steamboat. Onlookers mumbled and muttered, angry and impatient. The soldiers glared at the crowd, intent on keeping things in good order.

"Those braves are the pardoned prisoners," Joe pointed out. "Them and the women will be left off at Fort Snelling; from there they'll go to reservations along Crow Creek in Dakota Territory. I'll be moving my family there, to Fort Thompson." Soldiers on the paddle wheeler herded the two groups to areas fore and aft, then signaled for the next group. After another brief pause, a large contingent of prisoners—there looked to be near three hundred—hustled through the soldiers, apparently eager to get aboard. "These last are the ones Lincoln reprieved from hanging. They'll go to a prison camp in Iowa."

Not waiting for a reply, Joe clapped Johnny and Chaska on their backs and trotted toward the steamboat. "Come visit us in Dakota Territory," he called back.

Johnny looked at Chaska, whose expression was unreadable.

"What's the name of that paddle wheeler?" demanded a deep voice behind them.

"What?" Johnny turned to a gentleman in a black frockcoat writing with a charcoal pencil on a pad of paper. He must be a newspaperman. And he must have been listening to Joe, taking down his information. "Hey, mister, you can't . . ." Johnny began, then stopped when he heard whimpering. Emma clung to the man's pants leg, crying.

The reporter ignored her, craning his neck to see the steamboat. "The *Favorite*, is that it?" He scribbled on his pad. "What do you think, maybe four hundred boarded?"

Johnny knelt down and took Emma's hand. "What's the matter? Are you scared?"

Tears spilled out of her eyes and washed wet tracks down her cheeks. "Mama threw them in the fire." Emma threw back her ringlets and wailed. "She lifted off the lid on the cookstove and just shoved them in. Mama burned them up."

"The moccasins?" Johnny's chest tightened. Her mama burned them? He turned on his heels to look up at Chaska. Chaska was gone.

Johnny found him back at the wagon, adjusting Split Rock's light bridle.

"He won't take a bit," Chaska muttered through tight lips. "He doesn't need one, anyway." Tossing Johnny the reins, he spun around and leapt onto Lightfoot and galloped down the dirt street, scattering mud clods and pedestrians.

Johnny barely had time to grasp a handful of mane and jump onto Split Rock's bare back before the eager paint raced off after Lightfoot. "Tell Pa we went on ahead," he yelled back to Amy.

≈

The new spring leaves on the maples had sprouted and the windmill seedpods waited for a spring windstorm to scatter them. Johnny breathed deeply, savoring the smell of damp earth and wildflowers. His legs cramped a bit, stuck as he was on the wide tree branch. He wished Chaska would drive some game his way soon—it was danged uncomfortable sitting on a tree limb too long. Then nearby scuffling and scratching caught Johnny's ear. He sat quiet, listening.

Turkeys. Wary, wily game. Slowly he raised his rifle as the birds neared. Good thing they were close by; he didn't have a bird gun.

From the distance, a fox yelped, perhaps calling her pups, but likely it was Chaska, driving game his way. The entire flock of turkeys, now standing beneath Johnny's tree, raised their heads to listen. Johnny drew a bead on a big jake, long beard dangling down its chest. He fired.

Squawks and gobbles and flapping wings surrounded Johnny, great wingspans nearly clipped him off his perch. The turkeys quickly disappeared into trees and leaves.

Except the big jake, sprawled still beneath the tree. Johnny climbed down, hitting the ground as Chaska came trotting up the trail.

"Good shot," said Chaska, as he lifted the bird and spread its wings to gauge its size.

Johnny slung his rifle over one shoulder and the turkey Chaska handed him over the other. "At least it's easier to carry than a deer up a ravine," said Johnny.

The boys walked side by side along the burbling creek to the meadow. They sat on a fallen log to clean the bird, saving the feathers for Star Woman. Lightfoot and Split Rock grazed the sweet meadow grass nearby. The sun grew hot, the air sticky and humid.

Chaska cleaned his skinning knife with wet leaves he'd picked off the ground. He stood, sniffing the air, catching the direction and strength of the slight breeze. "It's too hot for this time of year. There will be storms today." He glanced at the horses pawing the ground. "The animals feel it coming."

Johnny stood, sniffing the air, trying to see and feel signs of an approaching storm. The air was muggy. The damp warm breeze seemed to be stilling itself. He wouldn't have noticed if Chaska hadn't called his attention to it.

"Star Woman tells of a great storm, when terrible winds collided. Great heavy heat had built up; animals and people felt its weight. The wind, the air, and the forest crouched still and silent, like animals that scent predators." Chaska scanned the sky, northeast to southwest like he expected something to pounce out of it. "Star Woman said the sun's light turned murky green, like scum on water, and suddenly the entire sky became a great black moving mass. It swirled and whirled and sucked up trees and rocks, even animals, into itself. What wasn't uprooted was shredded and destroyed. Little survived."

"A tornado," said Johnny. "Ma's seen them back in Wisconsin. The one Star Woman describes must have been huge."

"When powerful winds cross and crash against each other, it is terrible." Chaska looked from the still-blue sky to Johnny. "Like hatred and revenge, greed and power, I think the desolation those winds have wrought is beyond our power to restore."

Johnny swallowed hard, thought hard, struggling to lessen the grief in his friend's voice. "Look here, maple seeds." He reached down, scooped a handful, and tossed them in the air. "A few scattered seeds can grow strong and replenish a forest."

The maple seeds flitted down around them, one settling on Chaska's boot. Absentmindedly he scraped a small hollow in the dirt with his foot, nudged in the seed, and tamped loose soil over it. "Star Woman says the Dakota will return to this land one day. That many tribes of people will live together here in peace. She is wise and sees far, but it is hard to believe."

Johnny pointed to the little dirt mound covering the maple seed. "Do you believe a tree will grow there? That the Creator can call it forth and give it life?"

Chaska stared at the ground, just realizing he had planted a tree. "Yes, of course. It is the way of all things."

"Then let your faith extend to Star Woman's vision. Don't limit the ability of the Creator to repair what's been wounded." Quietness settled into the branches, sunlight softened. Distant thunder rumbled softly.

A demanding whinny rang through the meadow, startling Johnny and Chaska.

Split Rock pawed the ground, impatient. Lightfoot stretched his neck and echoed Split Rock's command.

"It seems our horses want to go home." Chaska hurriedly gathered a handful of scattered tail feathers, tucking them in his bag.

"Let's ride," said Johnny, hoisting the turkey over his shoulder and running across the meadow with Chaska. "We'll beat the thunderstorms."

AFTERWORD

Following the Dakota Conflict of 1862, about 800 Dakota (the war party) fled west to Dakota Territory. About 1,700 peaceful Dakota were confined near Fort Snelling and 300 convicted Dakota were imprisoned at Mankato.

Indian relocation became a major concern. Congress enacted laws that specified the war party Indians be relocated on unoccupied land beyond the limits of Minnesota. By June 24, 1862, the transfer of 1,300 Dakota and nearly 1,950 Winnebago (who had not participated in the war) was completed. Between 100-200 Dakota (the peace party) were allowed to remain. John Other Day was one of these.

Governor Alexander Ramsey kept a military presence throughout the state. Military expeditions into Dakota Territory pursued the hostile Dakota, fearing they would return and attack again. This grew into an extermination campaign, and bands that had not lived in Minnesota Territory or participated in the war in any way, were attacked and in some cases, massacred. These Dakota tribes, led by Red Cloud, Sitting Bull, and Crazy Horse, warred on the whites, and bloody battles resulted. The war that had begun at Acton in 1862 finally ended at Wounded Knee in 1890.

Chief Little Crow and about 150 of his band spent

the winter of 1862-1863 near Devil's Lake (North Dakota). In June 1863, Little Crow, his son, and sixteen braves returned to Minnesota on a horse-stealing raid. Little Crow was killed by farmers near Hutchinson on July 3, 1863. Chiefs Shakopee and Medicine Bottle were captured in Canada and given over to Fort Snelling, where they were hanged on November 11, 1865.

By the late 1880s, small numbers of Dakota began returning to Minnesota, settling near their old territories. They developed communities and farms. Dakota traditions and heritage thrive today in a proud and independent people.

ACKNOWLEDGMENTS

First and foremost, my heartfelt gratitude goes to Mary Casanova, who mentored me through a lengthy revision of this book. Not only is the book greatly improved by her critique, but her advice and encouragement greatly improved my writing abilities. Mary was Teacher, as well as Mentor.

Thank you to my editor, Gretchen Bierbaum, for her insightful revision suggestions and her generous approval and encouragement. Thanks also go to Susan Power, Dr. Don and Barb Olmanson, and Rick Allen for historical accuracy readings. This book was also enriched by family stories from Olga Preuss Neubert and Dr. Karolyn Hanna. And my appreciation goes to the Arts Center of St. Peter and The Night Writers, for encouragement and support.